CW00377169

Open Door

An Anthology

Hinckley Scribblers

Come on through our Open Door
Hope you'll all enjoy our store
And get a perk
From this our work,
Leaving you all wanting more.

C.R. 2023

Copyright for the following content is held by the
various writers accredited to the work © 2023.
All rights reserved.
ISBN: 9798858345152

Cover design by Sylvia J. Turner © 2023

Contributors:

Hinckley Scribblers is a face-to-face writers' group based in Hinckley, Leicestershire, UK. We meet weekly at the local library and seek to provide a friendly, supportive, informal environment for creative writers both professional and amateur. Our members include published, self-published and unpublished writers.

Contributors to this anthology are:

Creana Bosac
Norma Bowen
Bob Crockett
Farren
Cindie Hall
Brent Kelly
Anne Knapp
Sheila Lockett
Carol Mogano
Daven Potter
Peter Riley
Simon Rees-Jones
Olivia Robinson
Chris Rowe
Rita Stephens
Hugh Tibbits
John Trott
Sylvia J. Turner
John Welford
Rita Wilson

Contents

Relationships

Nature and Environment

Sci-Fi and Supernatural

... and Kitty Cried

Simon Rees-Jones

The blue of the sky burnt the eyes even when they were closed. The beat of the sun bore through the skull to torture the mind. The dust of the road billowed with each step, filling nose, mouth, ears, and eyes with grittiness. The scrape and shuffle of hundreds of feet, the click of thousands of crickets, the drones of millions of flies, none of them stopped to listen to the cry of a child.

The ebb of humanity was leaving its home in the foothills, driven not by the desire for a new beginning, but by certain knowledge that to stay was death. In the days and nights to come, they would walk and sleep in limbo; walk in the certain knowledge of sleep to come, sleep with no certainty of waking the next day.

Behind them, the village burned; the young men lay mostly still, but some twitched or slowly rolled in the dust as their blood dried in the dirt. The gunmen had gone too, onto the next village looking for more lives to destroy.

The people had built the village three months before, the third since they had left their homeland high in the mountains. They built it and waited for the rains; the rains never came, and the people didn't know how to live out of the dust of the foothills and the desert.

It wasn't the swollen bellies, the cracked lips, the empty breasts that made them go, that only meant possible death tomorrow. It was the guns, knives, and fire that meant certain death today that moved them.

The child cried again. She had seen six rains that came to the mountains, but in the desert, it hadn't rained for her. She had seen one brother with his brains in the dirt but hadn't stayed to watch another as the knives opened his body to the flies. She had walked with the cattle and watched them, with foaming mouths and hollow backs, fall into the ditch; a

2

needle could have saved them, but not here.

She had watched from behind her new home, her sister torn apart by men in sweaty uniforms, but had turned away as her father reached out from his burning body.

She had not cried for any of these things, it was her life, and she could not question it. Now she sat by the roadside and watched the people as they passed in silence, heads bowed, looking as far ahead as the next footfall.

The child turned to her mother and touched first the closed eyes and then the stiffening fingers. For the first time in her life, she saw tomorrow. The child's heart burst and Kitty cried.

Lifetime
Carol Mogano

I can't believe how time goes quickly by!
It speeds up as we age, I won't deny.
And aging's something we cannot control,
a process to endure until we die.

Well, few folk know for sure how long they'll live,
it's an unknown that's not our prerogative,
but life should not be measured by the years,
assessment should be more qualitative.

So live each day as if it were your last;
don't hold regrets relating to your past;
embrace the future, make each moment count,
you'll find the opportunities are vast.

Is It Me
Anne Knapp

Can you see me?

I'm not there.

You think you saw me on the stair.

Did you spot me in the crowd?

Was it me with my head bowed?

Is it me sat in that chair?

Take a look but please beware.

Is it me in that café?

Coffee and cake on loaded tray

you rush over to stand and stare.

Confronting a stranger's icy glare

is it me you glance upon that bus?

As I move away from all this fuss

you think you see me, now you don't.

I can't be seen as I'm not there

I'm sat at home in my old chair.

A Yearning
Farren

Jenny had a secret yearning for Blackpool. It wasn't the same place these days, but she had wonderful, magical memories of visiting as a child. Mum always laughing, Dad skimming stones, her brother Peter digging sand, trying to stop the tide's invasion of his crenelated castle, walking out for miles to reach the sea when the tide was out, potted shrimps, candyfloss, sweet and sticky, even the car journey home, sleepy and happy.

But this visit was a spontaneous decision made that morning when she awoke early and saw the sun shining. She just drove off and within ninety minutes she spotted the unmistakeable structure dominating the skyline. Parking on South Shore she walked with a spring in her step towards the Tower. It was still early and relatively empty of holidaymakers. A stall selling Morecambe Bay shrimps! An early lunch of potted shrimps. Wonderful! And so nostalgic. She looked out to see the sea, but the tide was out. Miles of empty sands with a few puddles reflecting the pale blue sky. She turned and went down the steps onto sands, kicked off her shoes and began walking towards the distant sea.

A man passed her in the opposite direction. He looked familiar.

"Lovely morning!"

"It is," she agreed smiling. He walked away whistling "Oh I do want to be beside the seaside, I do want to be beside the sea…"

"No-one whistles these days," she thought.

And suddenly she realised that he was the spitting image of her father, a much younger version than the old man foremost in her memory. This was Dad as a young man, in his twenties, probably before he was married.

"That would be around the late thirties just before the war," she mused.

Reaching the sea, the weather had changed, and the sky was grey. The water looked like slate, calm, hardly moving. She looked back over her shoulder towards the distant shoreline. She could still see the man. He appeared to be waiting at the bottom of the steps. She retraced her route unhurriedly. He was definitely waiting there. She felt a flutter of excitement, of concern, of disbelief.

As she approached, he stepped towards her. "I've been waiting for thee, lass. How about a candyfloss?"
Before she could reply there was a fearsome noise, a wailing, and somehow she knew exactly what it was. An air-raid siren! "But it can't be. This is 2020."

She looked for her father in panic, but her vision blurred. An explosion sounded close by, and she fell instinctively to the ground, curling into a foetal position. Next moment she was aware of peace and quiet and the kindly whisper of a nurse saying, "Wake up Jenny, just relax, you're OK, you fainted on the sea front. We've checked you out and wonder if you've eaten something unusual, shellfish perhaps?"

The Teardrop Slide Guitar Maestro

Sylvia J. Turner

'Lewis Brian Hopkin Jones.' What's the truth behind his story?

Found drowned, full of drink and drugs, devoid of any glory.

Fired, disgraced, cast-out, alone,

the founder of the Rolling Stones.

He'd placed an 'ad' in Jazz News, back in May Nineteen Sixty Two,

for 'talent,' his new band could use, in their Marquee Club debut.

It was early days. As founder, guitarist and the boss,

he planned to book the gigs and manage the show.

When asked 'what's the band called?' He was at a loss,

not quite prepared. He really didn't know!

'The Best of Muddy Waters' LP sleeve, lay discarded, on his bedroom floor,

The 'Rollin' Stone Blues!' did his eyes deceive?

Could he ever have prayed for more!

So Brian named the band 'The Rolling Stones.'

The group thought the name was brilliant.

Managing the band was left to Jones. He had the initiative and resilience.

He was a talented musician, even in his tender years,

outstanding slide guitarist, applauded by his peers.

This multi-instrumentalist had far to go!

It's his electrifying artistry that made 'Little Red Rooster' crow.

He embellished 'Ruby Tuesday,' with his woven music score.

The trills of his treble recorder framed her walking out the door.

Cover songs with their music layers, were magically transformed.

Simple lyrics, re-fashioned, with such artistry adorned,

with the unique, instrumental twists by Jones,

who put the meat onto the bones for the Rolling Stones.

Mick Jagger and Keith Richards were best school friends of old,

when Jones made band decisions, they didn't like being told.

Young immature men, they ganged up, and they bullied,

calling Brian bossy, abrasive, self-obsessive, sullied.

Brian's music was so complex, not just about a rhyme,

his instrumental timbre will haunt the annals of time.

He created drama with the reverberating buzz of his sitar, in 'Paint it Black.'

You hear his vocals and his Teardrop slide guitar on many a backing track.

His whistle in 'Walking the Dog' adds that special touch

unique little nuances that made fans love the Stones so much.

But Brian's love of music was never about the verse

yet, it was not writing many lyrics that became his fatal curse.

Brian Jones was far from perfect, his wild oats scattered without care,

at least six different girls had his babies, but none were his legal heir.

A torn, split personality, an angel and a devil

he really needed a helping hand, to keep him on the level.

He was a peacock, a gregarious extrovert, desperately seeking fame,

or, the thoughtful, self-deprecating introvert,

shy and sensitive, never to blame.

His rock band had now truly flourished,

found their fortune, made their name.

They hired a new manager who played a very different game.

Mick and Keith would write the lyrics and take the centre stage

leaving Brian feeling rejected, dejected, in his silent rage.

As sex and drugs and rock and roll, inevitably took their toll.

He finally lost his place in the band, his life, his love, his soul.

Depression, then the bleakness, the cruel grip of desolation,

self-doubt, and then the drug induced trap of his mental isolation.

He lost his sensibility, though he thought he was nobody's fool.

Drugs exacerbated his fragility, yet he always looked 'real cool.'

He became a slave to LSD, with no thoughts of impropriety,

adrift in his substance mist, a lost soul, floating free.

His ultimate demise he failed to see, his untimely death at his property.

Was it ever really meant to be?

They called it an accidental tragedy,

a twist of fate, you can't foresee. Now he's 'History.' His Story.

His musical ambitions were so complex, never just about a rhyme,

his Instrumental timbre will haunt the musical annals of time.

Found drowned, devoid of any glory. Stoned, disgraced, cast out,

washed up, alone.

The Teardrop Slide Guitar Maestro, the music man, the creator,

the first Rolling Stone.

Who knows his side of this story? Buried deep now, dead,

the truth unknown,

in a huge American coffin made of lead, they laid his bones,

Instrumental genius was his glory. The legacy of Lewis Brian Hopkin Jones,

multi-instrumentalist, slide guitarist and the founder of the Rolling Stones.

The Sanctuary
Cindie Hall

I need to promote the Sanctuary -
it's up and running eventually.

I thought a wristband
that's worn just above the hand.

A place to be
for all others to see.

Charge a little fee
I think people will agree.

You see, it's a place to meet
a real cosy retreat,

a place for peace
when you feel unease,

somewhere to heal
now that's a big deal.

Relaxation and meditation
I think there might be a staycation.

So, a small price to pay
to have all this come your way.

Happy and free
and that's the way it should be.

Apathy
Phil Whitmore

I really would like to be

a writer for radio & TV

but unfortunately

it's not to be

because of this cloud of apathy.

The apathy

of you and me

is not good for creativity

you see

it chokes and stifles me

this woeful cloud of apathy.

I cannot make a cup of tea

without this apathy

making me be

so down I frown you see.

I dwell in pits of misery

if only there were ways to be

successful & carefree

but curse this apathy

its strangulating me.

It's really,

really, really... (!!!)

Winning

Sheila Lockett

The breeze freshened and the sail billowed out. Roger felt the wind in his face and smiled. He was happy. His pride and joy, the new boat which he had picked up from the boatyard two hours earlier was everything he hoped she would be.

Since he had been a young boy, he had gazed with envy at the sailors as they raced across the Solent. It was wonderful to have the beach all year round, not just for holidays, but living in a cottage on the Isle of Wight, he knew that boats meant freedom. You couldn't get to the mainland any other way, well not unless you owned a light aircraft, not that he had any chance of that. Besides, he didn't like heights.

'Isn't this bliss Rowena?'

Rowena, looking a faint shade of green, didn't share his enthusiasm. She wished he hadn't won that golf tournament and decided that he owed her a new car now he had his new toy. No, she preferred solid ground under her feet.

'Could you drop me back to the harbour Rog, I don't think I can take much more of this.'

'OK love, you can wait in the cafe while I take her out for another trip. Or if you want to go home, take the car and I'll call you when I want picking up.'

'I might just do that; I feel like a lie down. You can stay out as long as you want.'

Roger felt rather pleased with this outcome; he could get to know every inch of his yacht. When he finally, reluctantly, took her back to her mooring, he couldn't resist taking a selfie. Roger with his yacht, he was determined to show it to his friends at the golf club. He angled the shot so that they would all be able to read the name of her too. That would rub a few up the wrong way.

It was a year ago that he had won the President's Cup at the club. He had known as he holed in one at the twelfth hole that unless he did something stupid, he was so far in front he couldn't help but win. Playing safely from then on, he had done it, won not only the cup but the generous prize money. His dream of owning a yacht could now become a reality, and what else was he to name her. The name Glorious Twelfth was painted in gold letters on the bow. Wonderful, Roger sighed, this was where he was meant to be.

Something to Cheer Us Up

Chris Rowe
October 2020

Outburst of orange by bright blue of sky,
Autumn's last blazon before the leaves die.

Outlook of long nights and power-cut days,
iced-up the windscreens and slow motorways.

Turmoil of landslide and blundering flood,
hail-strike and fog-fall and cloudburst and mud.

Concrete the landscape and chopped down the trees;
builders get richer, the North's on its knees.

Brexit with No Deal and HS2 rail:
Plans to bring profit - but what if they fail?

Don't do what I do but do as I say,
our rulers' mantra, while they're out at play.

Tough are the times now - how far can it go?
one day the country may stop and say No.

Covid's the foe now, our leaders can't cope;
faltering fades our faint glimmer of hope.

On the Chisholm Trail
John Trott

My father said, "It's time you got yourself a job of work and brung in some money or your gonna have to get out and feed yourself."

I was not surprised. I was thirteen and knew I should be able to help my family pay the bills. My mother told us, "Times are hard and there ain't no room for passengers."

Texas had supported the south in the war between the states and lost. We all suffered.

There were some Yankee carpetbaggers around who had plenty of money but none of the rest of us would speak to them. Anyway, we didn't have nothing and we had no money and had nothing worth selling. All I had to offer any boss was farm work and riding skills. I owned just my own old mare, but she weren't much use.

Jimmy McClintock came up with the answer. He was a year older than me and told me we could become cattle drovers. The cattle company would provide a string of horses for us to use. We would get paid thirty dollars at the end of the drive and all our victuals for as long as we worked for them.

I could hardly imagine such wealth.

The two of us rode into San Patricio and asked around and were told to go the saloon. Where agents were recruiting for a drive from the town to the stockyards at Abilene Kansas. We would be paid at the end of the drive and be gone for about five months.

But first we had to prove we could handle horses and cattle. The man in charge barked at us, "How old are you boys?"

I puffed out my scrawny chest, and in a voice that sounded far too young even to me, squeaked, "Fifteen sir."

He laughed. "Well if you can cut out that steer, the one with the black patch over one eye, I'll give you a job."

I wasn't bothered by his laughing because I knew I could do it. I've been doing it all my life.

I jumped on the nearest horse and did as he told me.
The man bellowed with laughter, "You'll do boy, you got the job." Then in a more serious voice, "We gotta drive the herd over seven hundred and fifty miles. You'll be in the saddle all day every day. You'll have to stop stampedes, fight Indians and kill to protect your money when it's all over. Do you still want the job?"

"That's why I'm here."

"My names Mark Jefferson I'm the foreman. Mr Jefferson to you."
And so it started.

I had been brung up the hard way and was never allowed to show fear when facing an angry steer. We would be driving the herd out onto the trail in two days' time. The following day my father arrived at the camp and found me.

"I ain't coming home," I shouted.

"I don't want you to," he hollered back. "I brung this for you, I figure you'll have more use for it than me and you're a better shot." He gave me a quick backslap and handed me his own gun, a Colt 45 and its holster.

"Look after yourself," he grunted. And without looking back he rode back out towards our spread.

Mr Jefferson laughed when he saw my gun. "Can you shoot that thing straight boy? I ain't running no dud outfit." I knew I could handle it and ignored the laughter.

The next morning, we started work.

By the end of the first day, I knew I was in for a hard time. Every muscle ached but it was no more than I expected. From then on, we worked all day and every day. Chasing down stubborn steers. Driving off coyotes, crossing streams and wondering why cattle are always looking for stupid easy ways to die.

Within a week we had all been accepted by the herd. And when they settled down at night, we reassured them by singing quietly, talking and whistling. The others said it was too good to last.

They were right. The next day the Indians appeared. Mr Jefferson was sensible. He didn't try to fight them off but offered three head of cattle in exchange for a safe passage, and eventually agreed to give them five and everybody was happy.

Days turned into weeks, and I was soon used to following the herd and breathing dust, and always working.

There were difficult times, like the big storm and a stampede when I got thrown and damn near trampled. I was lucky to escape. One of our crew got drowned crossing a river in Oklahoma. Then at long last we knew it would soon be over. There was more activity in the air and we first heard the faint sound of a train entering Abilene.

Mr Jefferson gathered us all round him. "We finish our journey tomorrow boys and our job is done. You will be paid off and the scum of the earth are waiting in line to rob you of every hard-earned cent. Look out for each other. Don't get stupidly drunk. Don't throw your money away on some flea-bitten whore. Most of all don't get into any fights, they shoot people around here."

We drove the herd into the pens and Mr Jefferson took us all to the edge of town. I was paid thirty-five dollars. It was more than I had expected. He advised us to catch the train east and return home on the Mississippi, but to stay out of Abilene.

There was a sudden sound of shooting and a drunken voice shouting, "This is a stick up." I think all of us drew our pistols and shot at him. Nobody made any big fuss and the drunk was buried. His name was Less Moore.

On his grave someone stuck a notice:

Here lies Less Moore

Shot to death with a forty-four

No Less

No More.

The University of Life
Carol Mogano

Your life's full of experiences, an overflowing pot.
Some you'll get to choose yourself, and others you will not.
They may be good, they may be bad, whatever you may do,
you'll realise the ones you've had have taught you something new.

Treat each one as a treasure, something sparkling and bright!
Think of it as an adventure like a trip, a trek, a flight.
Whether boring or exciting, even if you're filled with dread,
don't turn your back and run but meet it face to face instead.

If you sit and mope around at home just daydreaming and yearning
you'll miss the opportunity of experience and learning.
For experience is what we need, the teacher of all things,
and, like a bird, to see the world, you have to spread your wings.

You should make the most of every opportunity you get,
for nothing beats experience, and don't dwell on regret!
The things that turn out badly you can quickly throw away,
but the lesson that you've learnt from it should be allowed to stay.

It's the same if you're a grown-up or a little girl or boy,
there are always opportunities for new things to enjoy!
So, don't spend your time procrastinating, find something to do!
Look for a new experience, start learning something new.

Approach with positivity and expect it to be fun.
An optimistic attitude's best when all is said and done.
And when measuring maturity, our age we could discount
the sum of our experience is what should really count.

Rejected

Phil Whitmore

Send an e-mail, text, or call,
what good does that do?

None at all.

You wait and wait,
and truth be told,

you get rejected, not elected.

You try again,
such a pain,

and we're all getting old.

Invisible
Sylvia J. Turner

A true story

Christmastime, he walked through the noisy bar,
crowded, he's unnoticed, all on his own.
Just floating through, beneath the throng's radar,
he's totally invisible, alone.
Big Bill was big, but such a lovely guy,
a farmer, and a gardener, fit and strong.
Yet, no one even noticed him walk by,
that fateful night, his life had gone so wrong.
He was there, feeling, awkward, set-apart.
he questioned his existence, broke his heart.
Acknowledgement from his fellow man was all he really craved,
connection, if they'd nodded, smiled, or waved.
His isolated life brewed doubt and fear,
Bill had no time for weeping in his beer,
no time for drawn out self-diagnosis.
It turned into a damaging psychosis.
Dreams for his farm worker's cottage lay in tatters.
"Why would the Council think it even matters?"
He'd failed, his extension plans had been refused!
His needs ignored as insignificant; their powers abused.
This had been a lifetime's dream, his final goal
stripped from him like it was just a begging bowl.
He'd never confided to another living soul.
A doer not a thinker, that had been his role.
The Council wanted to tear his cottage down.
He was a farmer, it was on the farm, not in the town.
It was just after Christmas in Seventy-Eight
despite his persistence, they said they wouldn't wait.
He was so full of self-doubt, in despair,
when no one reaches out, who would really care?
He was questioning his own existence

his friends could have been there, to form resistance.
He had so much to offer, his great love of country life to share,
but others didn't notice him, like he wasn't there,
The next day when the news broke
'Big Bill Alsop' was found stone dead!'
Why did it ever come to that?
A shotgun blasted through his head.

History
and
Place

The Not So Good Old Days
Peter Riley

It's tempting when we hear of some of the horrors that surround us to imagine that some time ago there was a more serene, gentle and peaceful age. Today when we hear of football violence, we're tempted to think that in previous times people in crowds behaved themselves. When we work in a city or factory, we compare our situation with that of an imagined peaceful rural life of yesteryear.

We read of pollution by industrial waste, by the misuse of fertilisers on the land and we hark back to a time when everything was fresh and clean. We see a power station belching smoke and steam into the atmosphere and we dream of windmills and waterfalls.

It wasn't like that. Only two and a half centuries ago at the dawn of the industrial revolution the ordinary person had a life that was solitary, and according to Thomas Hobbes "nasty, brutish and short." Let's take a time capsule back to that era.

To feed himself a person had to toil all the daylight hours; when the dark came, he slept. Candles and oil were scarce, crops failed, and people starved. The only form of transport for the common man was 'Shanks' Pony' so he rarely travelled beyond the village and surrounding fields. The rare travel outside was hazardous and finding shelter unlikely. Only people living in a parish were entitled to stay there. The Lord of the Manor was the giver of life and death. Life for the ordinary person was harsh.

By an Act of 1670, a man had to be a Lord of the Manor to kill even a hare on his own land. The basic qualification to kill game was an income of 5 to 10 times the annual income of a labourer. Penalties for unqualified hunting were severe: five pounds fine or three months in jail for keeping a dog or snares; thirty pounds or a year in jail for killing a deer. Under the Black Act of 1723 transportation or death could be invoked at the pleasure of the Prosecutor if a deer had been killed in his parish.

On the order of the Earl of Uxbridge, who owned Cannock Chase, two labourers from Longdon were convicted and sentenced to death at Stafford Assizes in 1743 for killing two deer and a doe.

According to Bacon, the laws were necessary:
"to prevent persons of inferior rank from squandering that time, which their station in life, requireth to be more profitably employed." A law to protect the poor from their own idleness was said to be a 'salutary restraint.'

People made their position known by riot. The threat of riot meant that a peaceful gathering of the common man was unusual. Outside the town and village, the world was full of people escaping harsh justice. Few were Robin Hoods.

The sole source of energy was man's muscle and that of the animal if he could afford to feed it. Even in later times, when the miller had the assistance of a water wheel, the toll on human life was significant: in the dark, the mill pond claimed its victims. Maybe the drunkard deserved his watery death, but not the child playing at the water's edge. The village pond and the cesspit were sources of disease: pollution was not some remote fear but was on the doorstep. The kharzi at the bottom of the garden was a constant reminder.

Coming back to today, even in more recent times seemingly simple tasks were difficult. To import meat from the New World was a mammoth task. My grandad was a carpenter who went to Canada to seek his fortune building the Canada Pacific Railway. He returned when complete, rather than join the gold rush, working his passage on a cattle ship rebuilding the cattle pens in the bowels of the ship.

Food today is instantly available; we travel freely almost anywhere in the world; we can follow the life of others on the TV; we have power at the touch of a switch and the equivalent of a man's strength in a lightbulb. We are not concerned about where the next meal comes from but with remote perceived hazards: small traces of chemicals from an incident far away or the effect of acid rain on remote forests.

We have a clean, relatively smoke free environment, we have leisure time and to quote Harold MacMillan "We've never had it so good."

Old Pop John
Bob Crockett

My Great-grandfather John passed away in 1980 at the age of ninety. I was twelve at the time and I remember his funeral very well. My sister and I called him Old Pop, to distinguish him from our father who we just called Pop, never Dad. He was always cheerful was Old Pop. People said it was being so "bleeding cheerful" that kept him going for all those years. And it was true, he was a man who radiated good cheer despite everything that happened in his life. He was good company at home and amongst his many friends. A real glass-half-full man, never half empty. He always looked on the bright side, even when Millwall lost!

He'd been a soldier in the First World War and then, in the Second, when he was too old for soldiering, he did his bit as an ARP warden, going around telling people to "Turn that Light Out" like Warden Hodges, the permanently aggrieved grocer in Dad's Army. "He's my favourite character," he used to say. "I was just like him during the war wasn't I Queenie?" And his wife, my Great-grandmother Lisbeth would laugh and say, "No, more like that Captain Mainwaring. A right little Napoleon you were, always blowing that bloody whistle of yours." And then someone would say, "His trumpet more like!" and we'd all laugh.

He used to talk a lot about the war and his life working in the docks. I loved to hear his stories and ignored the fact that, as he got older, he would tell the same story over and over again. But there was one story he didn't like to tell, and that was what really happened to my grandmother Marjorie who died just before the war ended.

In fact, it wasn't until Covid took my own mother Violet, or Vi as she was known to all, that I learnt the full story. Mum had inherited her grandfather's optimistic outlook on life and kept saying to me, "Don't worry Johnny. We'll get through this just like we did in the war. You know me, I always hope for the best." Sadly, she didn't make it, and while sorting through her papers I came across something that Old Pop

John had written before his hands became too shaky to hold a pen. In part, it was his recollections of the terrible V2 rocket attack on the Woolworth's store at New Cross, London on the 25th November 1944, which killed 168 people and left many more injured both physically and mentally. I knew he had written about it before for the local newspaper and had even sent something to the BBC but in this particular account, which he addressed to my mother, he revealed how the horror of that attack had affected my Grandmother Marjorie.

On the day in question, Old Pop was in the Marquis of Granby with some of his work mates. Around 12.30 p.m. they heard a loud noise like a 'crump' sound and then a massive explosion that shook the building and sent glass from the windows flying across the pub.

The air seemed to be sucked out of their bodies. Once they'd got their breath back they'd gone outside and saw the appalling carnage the rocket had caused. On the yellowing pages, he'd written:

> *"There was a huge crater where Woolies had been and blood and bits of bodies everywhere. We all got roped in to help clear the mess and look for casualties. Then I remembered that Marj had said she was going to go down to Woolies because there was a rumour they had some new saucepans come in and I thought, 'I hope to God she didn't have the kids and Queenie with her.' I started scrabbling away at the debris like a madman. I was desperate to find them, hoping and praying they were OK. Then I saw her. She was standing in the middle of the road covered in dust with little Stanley beside her. She looked stunned and lost and the poor kid was bawling his eyes out.*

> *Eventually, she managed to tell me that they had to stop on the way to Woolworth's so Stan could use a toilet. She was just on her way to the store when it got hit. I asked her where her mother and little Vi were and she said they were back at home because Vi had gone down with a cough. I got her away from that place and back to the house but she was never the same afterwards. Nor was little Stan. He never left his mother's*

side from that day one. Both of them would jump at the slightest sound and start shaking. It didn't help that we had no idea what had happened to Arthur (my grandfather) since Singapore had fallen. Queenie and I kept hoping against hope that Marjorie would rally round if only for the children's sake but she just got worse. We got some pills off the doctor but they were no use.

Then not long before VE day, it happened. They'd lifted some of the blackout restrictions by then and we had what we called the 'Dim Out.' That only allowed us to have the same level of light as a half decent moon so there still wasn't much to see by. But we knew it would all be over soon and we could start getting back to normal. Like it was before the war only better.

That night in April '45 little Stanley was particularly troubled and was constantly screaming and crying. In the end, I couldn't stand it anymore and got up and went into her room. I wasn't feeling too clever myself and I was tired and irritable. I said to her, 'If you can't get him to sleep you'll have to go elsewhere. Both of you! I can't stand it anymore. Some of us have to work you know!' And then I went back to bed. Of course, I didn't mean it. Then I heard her get up and go downstairs. I thought she might be making a cuppa. I fancied one myself so I got up and went down after her.

Before I got to the bottom of the stairs I saw her walk out the front door with Stan in her arms. He was still crying. She walked right out into the road and straight into the path of an army truck. They both died instantly. It was put down to sleepwalking while under the stress of the war and separation from her husband. That it was just a tragic accident and she hadn't meant to kill herself and the boy but I have never got over the feeling that it was my fault. That my angry words had tipped her over the edge. People always say to me, 'John, how come you're always so bleeding cheerful?' And I say, 'Well you have to be otherwise you'd top yourself'."

The rest of the note contained words of affection that showed how much he and Queenie had loved the little girl who woke up to find she had lost her mother and brother and would soon find out that her Daddy wasn't coming home from the war.

I've kept the letter and I`m waiting for the right moment to show it to my sister. She's had her own problems of late. I'm hoping they'll get sorted out soon. So, I'll keep it to myself for now, just as my mother kept it to herself for all those years. Old Pop must have written it for Mum in the hope of getting some sort of closure for the both of them. That and as a way of explaining why he was always so "bleeding cheerful," despite everything that happened.

The Soldier

Norma Bowen

In isolation he stood on the kerb,
though there were many people around him,
he called out for help but nobody heard,
they passed him by with a look of forbidding.

With a runny nose and smelling foul,
and his unfastened boots looking shoddy,
his aching bones brought him to howl,
as he struggled with his misshapen body.

A decade before he was man of the house,
he was trusted, loved and respected.
His offspring have gone and so has his spouse,
but it was said that it was expected.

The blame they say was the war in Iraq,
and the injuries he sustained.
He wasn't the same when he came back,
minus an arm, though he never complained.

The liquor went down to ease the pain,
from the nightmares of rocket attacks.
He sold his watch to a man in the rain,
to take shelter in the old barracks.

In isolation he stood on the kerb,
with an unsteady gait and a stutter.
He called out for help but nobody heard,
as he reached for his medal in the gutter.

Part of the Plan

Peter Riley

The post-war development of South Korea was disrupted until the revolution of 1961, following which the military government resolved to pursue industrial development and, while there was increasing western involvement, it was not a country that generally suited the western diet. This project would involve large numbers of western engineers and families over many years from the late sixties to the late seventies and food had to be part of the plan. Description of the project that I would be happy to relate with all its complications is for another day. Let it suffice to say, it was a venture between British engineering and civil engineering companies to build the first nuclear power plant in South Korea that was to be supplied by American and British companies under contract to the Korea Electric Co.

Initially the provision of food was not a problem, as most of the pre-contract and early preparations involved investigations, negotiations and meetings with the customer, contractors, and commercial organisations. Hotels and restaurants were able to cater for western tastes and to introduce westernised Korean style foods, Japanese and Chinese foods that many westerners could accept. For the more conservative, American food was always on the menus. A large U.S. army was deployed in the country so the occasional treat in the officers' mess was enjoyed.

The supply of western type food was of pivotal importance in the isolated location of the project. To the nearest area of westernisation, the city of Busan, was a two-hour car journey over sandy, bumpy roads and across forded streams. The local villages catered only for Korean taste and the cleanliness of the local vegetables was questionable, being irrigated with fluids from the cesspools fed from both animal and human excrement. Probably the only safe vegetable was Kimchi, a cabbage and root crop chopped and preserved then stored in clay urns over winter to ferment buried in the frozen earth. The result was the production of a pickled cabbage high in vitamins, low in fat, with no cholesterol but with a bitter taste that most westerners take time to accept.

For the construction of the project, an expatriate staff prepared to serve on two-year contracts was essential to maintain the high quality of supervision and training of the local contractors. Similarly, to maintain reasonable standards of behaviour, a stable family situation was to be encouraged by having suitable living conditions, recreation, schooling for juniors, a nurse with basic facilities and local provisions. The provision of a regular supply and facilities for dispersal of western food was essential and contractual arrangements had been made to allow the import of provisions on a regular basis.

Work started on site in the Autumn of 1971 near the fishing village of Ko-Ri, with a small team of civil engineers and two families to be joined before Christmas by myself and family and one other mechanical engineer. The first group of houses were ready and furnished, along with a kitted Bachelor Quarters (BQ), school room and recreational area, and the perimeter of the camp was secure with a guard post. The first shipment of provisions had not cleared customs and the size made it so apparent that the 'usual' methods were not effective.

A resourceful civil procurement manager had sourced the shops around Busan and was able to satisfy the immediate needs, but with Christmas coming and the threat of isolation due to snow on the two high passes, all effort was concentrated on gathering stock. By special intervention, the customer and the local police chief arranged for the release of the shipment, but clearly this was a one off until the import licence was cleared: this took over a year. A pleasant and memorable Christmas was enjoyed.

Until the licence was cleared, a range of ways were followed to procure food: the markets of Busan proved to be reliable suppliers to the existing international community, including a strong German technical educational unit, an international commissary accessible only by passport that was stocked with mostly American provisions but in amounts that would be exhausted with the expected peak of over two hundred on the camp.

Our wives organised weekly visits, where one of the Korean drivers had a contact with a contact who knew a Korean wife of a US serviceman who had access to the post exchange (PX), a US army shop: it became a routine to select the week's provisions from the PX list, leave it with the driver and the ladies would go for lunch at the Seamans Club, to be met later by the driver with a boot full of boxes of stuff. Our ingenious procurement manager found ways of keeping the bachelor kitchen provided that included a Hong Kong trader who had access to an import licence and a source of a powerful cheese from a monastery in the nearby mountains.

The import licence was cleared after a year or so, but selected foods were always difficult to find, so visitors and new recruits were always tasked with bringing specific presents and later, when heavy equipment was being shipped direct to the site dock, the Captain also carried our order of special cheeses and wines as arranged with our head office. That arrangement lasted for about six months, until the Korean site superintendent advised that we were risking further customs problems if the press got wind of activities.

Domestic life settled down into the usual routines, with the occasional excuse for a party when a visiting official, company boss, the local Anglican missionary, the Ambassador and his entourage, potential buyers for nuclear plants and so on came to the site. In the winters it was more likely a trip with one of our US engineers who had served in the forces to the Officers Club in Busan.

On rare occasions our Korean contractors would take us to a traditional Korean restaurant, and we had the opportunity to visit other parts of South Korea. Our home leave after two years took us on a month-long route home with the opportunity to sample the delicacies of several countries. We returned to a well-stocked and populated camp with the shell of 600 MWe power plant and back to work, except that this time we had with us a small person who had been made in Korea.

Now, over fifty years later, South Korea is fully industrialised. It has become a major car exporter and has sold nuclear power stations to the UAE and potentially to Poland. Korean spicy Kimchi dishes are available here. The Korean health care support has much to teach us.

The Plague Carrier's Tale
Bob Crockett

*Recalling a previous 'unprecedented' time when the Black Death,
sometimes called the Pestilence or the Great Mortality, swept through Asia
and Europe in the 14th Century AD killing millions. It is estimated that over
three million people died in the British Isles.*

From Gascony, I took most urgent leave
to flee fair Aquitaine and foul disease.
And from King Edward's endless foreign war
in France's fields smeared red with limbs and gore.
With riches torn from violated wives,
I'll buy Papal pardons for Paradise,
the sooner my Heavenly Lord to see
by spending less time in Purgatory.
But before my ship could prepare to sail,
a passenger joined me, his pallor pale.
A scrofulous air hung about his frame
and I feared that my soul he'd come to claim.
From a black fur coat more alive than he,
a rank, pustulous arm reached out to me.
"For company," he said, "A tale I'll tell
of my deadly journey through scenes from Hell,
In lands where the Devil scorned those who wept
and God and all his Saints their silence kept.
In Tartary, I ran my deadly course.
of Cathay's many woes, I am the source.
My bubonic crusade has been their bane
and great multitudes there my bite has slain.
Painful death I brought to the great Khan's court.
Porous, his mighty wall availed him nought.
Shahs and Sultans are now in my power.
Empires tremble and Holy Men cower.
Byzantium enticed my contagious trade.

Now, through corpse-strewn streets its Emperors wade.
When Sicily refused my advances,
I seduced her with infectious glances.
Through Italy my pestilential breath
engulfed her cities in foul clouds of death.
Noisome pus oozed from armpit, groin, and thigh
from fevered bodies, I condemned to die.
And through the courtly realms of Spain and France
it was I who led out the macabre dance.
The pious German prays and incantates,
then with whips and sticks, self-flagellates.
Christendom cries out, 'Jesus, please forgive
our sins so we may forever live.'
Now to England, I'll make my pilgrimage
and fright serf and lord with my grim visage.
In tribute a million poor souls I'll take
but you I will spare for our friendship's sake.''

Crime
and
Mystery

Real Crime
Rita Stephens

He never imagined that night that he would fall in love - a feeling that had eluded him in two failed marriages and several short couplings, where lust had been the driving force. This unexpected encounter, with an emotion that had carefully sidestepped him, came about at the book launch - his book launch to be precise.

How he hated the tediousness of those events. Success had not brought him contentment. His passion for writing had long faded, eroded by his need to churn out every year one formulaic crime blockbuster that seemed to soar up the league table of must-reads as soon as it hit the shelves. Guaranteed success, as his agent constantly emphasised, should not lead to complacency.

He still had to have book launches, to sit in draughty shop fronts doing signings for the great Aunt Agathas, to travel the length and breadth of England taking the red eye, to be followed by clichéd question and answer sessions, pandering to the middle classes who all thought they had a book inside them to write. All this, as well as keeping up a social media presence, was taking its toll. He now had thousands of followers as his agent kept on telling him.

On this night, he felt pimped out by his agent. His most recent idea for a book had been strongly rejected by her. 'Stick to what you are good at. You can't let your readers down.' She had looked at him authoritatively.

"Take it from me, if you try and move into a different genre, you'll be at the bottom of the wood pile again."

The woman that had caught his attention, at the book launch, had been standing holding a flute of champagne, arm outstretched which, to the waiter going past, appeared as a request for a refill. A more discerning observer, like himself, would have guessed that the stance was merely to put some distance between her and a rather obnoxious little man who was trying to look down her cleavage.

The glint of gold on her wedding finger had not deterred him from moving in swiftly, telling himself that he was rescuing a damsel in distress, rather than responding to the magnetic pull that made him sidestep all the passing greetings to stand beside her. She had turned, and with one smile he had been captured.

That evening, he left his book launch early but not alone. They had shared tapas at a nearby bistro, and talked until they were forced to leave when the impatient waiters dimmed the lights. They arranged to meet the following day, and then the day after until they found the day became the night, and by then they both had declared their love. When he asked her to get a divorce and marry him, she was distraught. 'I can never leave my husband. I am all that he has. He would die if I left him.'

She argued that they could be very happy together as they were. 'Listen my darling, my literary agency wants to work with you. That is a very good reason for me to come to England. France has a great demand for the English writer, and if you decide to let me have your books translated, it will not seem strange if we meet here or in France. Just imagine, Cheri, every time we meet up would be like a second honeymoon.' Her French accent flowed sensually, dulling his disquiet at being denied a yes to his marriage proposal. He was smitten, knowing full well that he would have to settle for whatever crumbs fell from her table.

On his now frequent trips to France, he had been introduced several times to her husband. Colourless was the way he summed him up. A man that liked his own company and followed a routine rigidly, taking his morning stroll, tending his garden, and then writing weighty academic tombs that few people read.

Discontentment had driven him into action. Being a crime writer, all the research he needed had been carried out in his books. He had breathed in the seedier side of the big cities, sat in police cars, visited prisons, and tapped into the dark web; he knew all the twists and turns needed to ensure that the criminal was not caught.

He made his contacts in Manchester. There was always someone, for a hefty fee and a one-week's break in France, who would do the deed. He supplied a recent photograph of the intended victim, the location, and a detailed account of the man's movements. He chose a weekend when he knew his lover was in Paris for a book launch. He was sure it would be chalked up as a burglary gone wrong. He bought a burner phone, arranging for a call to be made once the hit was carried out.

The call came in on the Monday morning. A Mancunian accent stated that the job had been done.

"Are there any problems I should know about?"

"Not really," he hesitated slightly before saying, "the thing is his wife, quite a tasty bit of stuff, appeared. I am afraid she got a good look at me."

"Don't worry, it is unlikely she will recognise you. They, no doubt, will be looking for someone from France. I hope you were wearing gloves and cleaned up after you?"

"Oh, don't worry about that, I got rid of her as well so there ain't no witnesses."

He did not hear the voice say, "Sorry mate," as he keeled over and vomited as the old cliché of 'crime does not pay' flitted achingly across his mind.

The Wheel Came Off

John Trott

The wheel came off the supermarket trolley and that was what saved me. I bent down to try and fix it, just as a tin of tomatoes exploded over my head, soaking my face, head and shirt front with bright red tomato juice. The tin didn't just spontaneously explode, the bullet hit it instead of hitting my head. I fell to the floor feigning death and heard the sound of running feet as my attacker made his escape.

Then people started screaming and I heard a guy say, "Is he dead?" I rolled over, climbed to my feet and tried to play dumb. "What happened there?"

The guy said, "He tried to shoot you, I saw the gun and he had a silencer." Then he shouted, "Call the cops, there's been a shooting." I knew I had to get out quick or I'd spend the night being questioned by the police, so I ran for it.

I had expected some retaliation, but never thought Maggot Mullinder had the guts to authorise a hit in broad daylight. I had underestimated him. I had only got out of the Scrubs two days ago and what's the first thing I do when I get out? I upset the local gang boss: not the brightest thing I've ever done.

I had been away for three years and, although I had an idea what was going on, I had lost touch with most of the old crowd. So, when I got out, I thought I would see who was about. The Blind Beggar was the place to go, so about nine o'clock I wandered in and saw a few faces I knew and got talking. I soon knew who was in, who was out and who was a grass. Then I noticed a group of three walk in, two really big guys and a little one, but you could tell who was in charge. The little guy had a real swagger. Then he turned and looked directly at me. I didn't believe it, it was Maggot Mullinder and I thought, 'What does he think he's doing with two heavies, he's just a little thief?'

So I turned to Arnie next to me and said, "What's up with Maggot? How come he's got that pair trailing round after him?"

Arnie looked pale all of a sudden, "Don't call him that, we call him Maggsie now and he's the one running the firm."

So I said, "Maggot in charge, I heard some rumours in the Scrubs but I never believed it. How could you let that little weasel take over?"

Arnie just shook his head. "Things have changed since you went down Dave, he's a crafty little sod and ruthless with it. Just make sure you don't upset him."

I shook my head. "It can't be true."

Anyway, I soon got talking to a few others and with me being just out of nick they all bought me drink or two, and a bit later I realised I was well on the way to being drunk. I couldn't hold it the way I used to. So I wandered outside to try and clear my head, and who should follow me out but Maggot?

He says, "Hello Dave, nice to see you're out, but a word of warning, you don't do any jobs on this manor without my say so and I expect ten percent off the top, got it?"

I staggered back a step and stared, thinking: 'Has he no respect, who does he think he is telling me what I can and can't do, and he wants a cut the cheeky bugger.'

He spoke again, a harder tone this time. "Are we clear?"

So I says, "No we ain't bloody clear, as far as I'm concerned Maggot, I do my jobs when and where I want and I keep the proceeds; one hundred per cent."

He smiled without humour. "I always knew that mouth of yours would get you in trouble one day Dave, and its Maggsie now not Maggot, I don't like that name."

So swaying a bit and angry, I raised my voice. "I'll call you Maggot if I want, I can't believe they let you take over, they must be getting soft." That smile again. "I'll get a couple of my associates to come and have a word with you, they can advise you who runs the manor now."

I was feeling really drunk and brave by now, so I slapped him round the head, told him to sod off and then I jumped in a taxi.

Next morning, I found out just how much I'd screwed up when Arnie came round.

"Look Dave," he said, "Maggsie knows you were drunk and he's willing to go easy on you. You just have to go round to his club by twelve o'clock and apologise and his lads will give you a smack or two, nothing drastic, just so he can say you've had a lesson and shown some proper respect. OK?"

I told him yes, fair enough, and as soon as he was out the door I packed my bag and headed out. He was taking me for a mug and there's no way I was going to volunteer for a kicking. As I scarpered, I thought I would just have time to get a couple of essentials from the supermarket and, well you know what happened.

I was in deep trouble and I knew it: I needed a plan. I had nowhere to run and no money. My problem is that I am an honest man and an honourable villain. I don't rob old ladies in the street, I don't go in for violence in public and bring the law storming into the neighbourhood upsetting people and I never, ever grass. It's not only my sense of duty that prevents me from grassing, but also my personal knowledge of what happens to grasses when they get found out.
I assessed my options.

I could try and get a few of the old mob together and displace Maggot. But I knew the group of ordinary thieves that I know would never go up against the heavies Maggot had got together. I've been out of touch too long and Maggot was obviously well in charge now and I knew he wouldn't forgive me for disrespecting him.

I could move out of the area and lay low, but with no money I would have to stay visible and there were too many people who would tip off Maggot just to stay in his good books.

Or; I could do the unthinkable and become a grass. Not one of the low lives who keep running to the Old Bill and grassing up all and sundry for the price of a couple of drinks. No, I should be a proper grass, a supergrass. New name, new start away from London and enough money to set myself up in business, an honest business of course, at least at first.

At the Blind Beggar I'd found out enough to keep Maggot locked up for years. There were two bodies the Bill didn't have a clue about and a stash of nicked jewellery in a safety deposit box in the west end.
I was soon on the phone and arranged for a meet with Detective Inspector Phil Pledger. He was the one who got me the three stretch, and I know he's an honest copper, so I didn't hold it against him. It didn't take us long to come to an agreement.

The deal was that I would feed the Old Bill everything I knew about Maggot. I would not have to give evidence in court, because I'd only passed on what others had told me, although I would have to say who told me. But I'm not stupid and nor are Maggot and his mates. It would take them about five minutes to work out who the grass was, and I would never be able to show my face in London again.

I'm told the weather is better in Devon and Dorset. I might have a try at living down there.

Jigsaw
Farren

She noticed it lying under another. It had a straight edge and that was
what she was searching for. The last piece needed to complete the
outside edge of the jigsaw. It was the way she worked, a tried and
trusted method. She'd always enjoyed jigsaws from just a young child. Of
course, as she grew older, they became more complex, at least a
thousand pieces, and the rule she applied was never to look at the
picture on the box until completion.

Edwin had always encouraged her by including one puzzle every year
amongst her Christmas presents. She would savour the wrapped
unopened box until after twelfth night and then begin. For about a week
in the dark days of January it would engross her, using up all her spare
hours until finally she would cry out, "Eureka," calling to Edwin that it
was complete. "Champagne!" he would respond and crack open the
bubbly.

And every year the same pleasurable routine. That is, until ten years ago
when one night in January Edwin disappeared. Such a shock for her. He
just went out that morning as usual, kissing her goodbye, and never
came back. That night around midnight she had contacted the police and
when they had asked all the questions and checked all possible contacts
and locations, they put out a missing person's alert. She was in limbo for
six days and then inexplicably his car and briefcase were discovered in
woodland close to Loch Ness. Not a place either of them had ever visited
as far as she knew.

With no explanation the police were unable to come to any conclusions,
but a few days later a damaged dinghy washed up on the far shore with
his shoes and jacket tangled on the floor. Inside the jacket was his wallet
and passport. Was it suicide, a mental breakdown, murder?

The police came back then and meticulously checked the house, computer, telephone records, bank statements and other financial transactions. Nothing untoward appeared. Bereft and with no close family, she relied on friends and neighbours for support, The company he worked for as an accountant were kind and continued to pay his salary for 3 months but without a death certificate pensions, death in service benefits and life insurances could not be sorted out.

She went to Citizens Advice who explained that around 250,000 people go missing in the UK each year of which 98% come back within a week and half of the remainder re-surface or are found within the first year. On this basis, no insurance company will pay out quickly. The general rule is that after seven years you can apply for the missing person to be declared dead but even then, it may take two or three years for it to be confirmed.

So, she went back to work and managed a frugal existence, still paying off the re-arranged mortgage. Not many luxuries but she always bought herself a big jigsaw every Christmas. Finally, after seven years, with the help of the charity Missing People, she did apply and eventually obtained life insurance and pension rights. It had been so long that it came as much as a shock as when he disappeared. Now she could give up work, but she didn't. She liked the colleagues she worked with, the contacts and camaraderie. "No going back," she thought. And having struggled with the mortgage all these years she felt free and decided to downsize to a small bungalow. A new start. It felt good!

Just a week in her new home and with Christmas on the horizon, she planned to do her Christmas shopping that morning. But as she went to get the car from the garage the postman arrived with a parcel. She thanked him and took it back inside. As she removed the brown wrapping paper she felt a cold breath, a shiver of her body. For there was a see-through plastic bag in which she could see a mass of jigsaw pieces.

She sat down, took a deep breath, and opened it. No message, nothing. The wrapping paper showed a UK stamp, postmarked London. This jigsaw was not going to be kept until after twelfth night. She poured the pieces out onto her dining table and began by sorting out the straight edges.

After finding that last piece of edge to complete the rectangle, she sorted the pieces into colours. A lot of light browns, dark browns, many with gold lettering. It took her all day. As she progressed the picture emerged of a polished bookcase of just two shelves filled with large dark brown leather volumes with gold embossed titles. Top shelf in order was Pickwick Papers, Oliver Twist, Nicholas Nickleby, The Old Curiosity Shop, Barnaby Rudge, Martin Chuzzlewick and Dombey and Son.

The novels of Charles Dickens, books she loved. Then underneath the sequence continued with David Copperfield, Bleak House, Hard Times, Little Dorrit, A Tale of Two Cities, Great Expectations, Our Mutual Friend and finally a book without a title, the final piece missing. She looked around but the floor was bare, the packaging empty. Then suddenly she remembered what she should have known all along. The Mystery of Edwin Drood, Charles Dicken's final unfinished novel. He was still out there somewhere and now, he wanted to come home.

Milkmaid
Hugh Tibbits

Rosetta has no time for me, she's busy running errands. There again, why would she, me a hawker, she a milkmaid, but a boy can dream. I've messaged her, reminded her I am crazy about her, that I'd do anything for her. She hasn't replied.

Kingfisher is swooping in later with new supply, a cut above the street-norm it's rumoured. Punters will love it; some will die happy, some'll be left baying at the moon.

She wasn't always lost. I knew the girl she once was; a communion dress, an early riser, a late night star gazer. I'd held her hand by Tesco's in the rain. She'd a future planned, diplomas, travel, aiding an ailing world; that all before the downfall she'd procured from Captain Cal, he bigger and stronger than I will ever be. He purchased the deeds to her future with a single wrap, an eye opener, a ticket to Fuddleworld.

Milkmaids see to everything, to everyone's needs, so at least she's realised part of her dream; her helping hand. Captain Cal lives in the bigger place, rides fast and furious, bleeds rich. Rosetta, jettisoned, finds solace in servicing others. She's a favourite of the Southside crew, bossed by Falcon. They keep her busy.

I sometimes see her parent-folks out looking; always looking. Posters strung on trees, pleas on media for information leading to their reconciliation. Rosetta's too far gone to see or hear them. I divert their attention with crumbs, cold comfort, but a scent is a scent even when it's a false trail. 'Better to be doing than fretting' my grandad would say as he worked at his lathe.

I'm on the corner of Willington and Thorndyke, a pocket full of mumble left to hawk. We work tight protocols, keeps us vigilant. I'm selling to a guy in glasses when I see Rosetta boarding a motor by the jewellers on Murdoch Street. She's acting cool but, because I know every inch of her,

I can tell she's running scared, which is unlike her because she's normally so fearless. The car takes off. It belongs to Merlin from Westside.

Milkmaids have a price. I heard Falcon wasn't prepared to meet hers. Rosetta, dead, is discovered out by Birchwood, squeezed into a rusted churn, her eyes left for the crows.

Me?
Oh, I'm okay.
Time is tight on the corners so no time for crying over spilt milk.

Countdown *[12.45]*
Simon Rees-Jones

The phone has been ringing for at least three minutes on a desk where nobody sits. Next to the phone is a cold coffee-ringed Snoopy mug, a Whitbread ashtray, and a crumpled pack of ten Embassy.
The Casio wall clicks another digit over.

11:17, Monday March 1st .

Still the phone rings.
It is the only phone ringing in the office, where stands five ink and tea-stained wooden desks, each with their own detritus, three occupied by white males, mid-thirties, in varying degrees of shiny suited, shabby disinterest. At the fourth is their senior officer, older, shabbier, no more interested. By a battered green filing cabinet stands a bright eyed, mid-twenties, uniformed WPC. The empty desk with the unanswered phone stands under the rain-streaked window, with a craned-neck view of the grey river below.

11:19.

Still the phone rings.
"Hey, blondie, get me a coffee, and pick up that bloody phone!"
Click. Scarf over the mouthpiece, breathe slow, don't panic. Just read the message.
"Martha says you need to clear Pope Street."
"Hello, Greater Manchester Police, can you repeat that?"
She sounds young – maybe even younger than him. Just not as scared – yet.
"This is Martha, clear Pope Street – now – please."
Under the clock, at the once empty desk, she looks across at her boss.
"Who's Martha?"
"Say again blondie?"
"Martha says we have to clear Pope Street."

Clock clicked.

11:23.

"Get the coffee love, it's just some nutter."
Through the scarf he tries again.
"Did you hear me? Martha says clear it now."
Then, softly.
"You have to. Please."
"Coffee sweetheart, NOW!"
She jumps, rattles the receiver in the cradle, scrapes the chair back, scurries to the little kitchen.
The grey scarf, now bundled in a ball, sits on the shelf above the 'A' button, his receiver back on the hook.
He turns in the urine stench, back to the scratched and foggy window that blurs his view of the damp street, grey in its winter cloak.
'Park the van outside the post office' he'd been told, 'It'll look like you're dropping parcels off.'
And there it still sits, fifty yards away, engine ticking as it cools in the Mancunian drizzle.
He turns his wrist to check his Ingersoll.

11:53.

Still cars stop, start, and splash on – past his telephone box, down Pope Street to pass the grey van. With coffees placed on the desks of her boss and the rest of the team, she sits down at the empty desk. Not her desk yet; she is new, raw, keen – not yet shabby and jaded. Not yet part of the team.

As she tips the acrid ashtray over the battered tin bin, the phone rings out again.

12:11.

"Have you put the warning out?"
"Who is this please?"
"It's bloody Martha, don't you understand?"
"I really don't. I'm sorry, are you in some sort of trouble?"
"We're all in bloody trouble if you don't get everybody away from the Post Office."

"Where are you?"
She's trying to trace me… can they find out where the call is from? They didn't warn me about that. Phone down.
Out into the damp day.

12:16.

"It was that bloke again, about Martha, we have to clear everybody away from the Post Office."

12:17.

Mug bang down on his desk, more coffee stains. Heads turn. Silence.
Realisation dawns through the slow, lazy cigarette smoke.
"Martha? Shit, the code… which Post Office?"
"Pope Street?"
"Fuck… what time?"
"He didn't say a time."
"They're supposed to give us a time, think blondie, what bloody time did he say?"
"I'm sure he didn't say – when he rang before he just said 'now'."
"Shit…," nicotine finger pointing, shaking, "You – bomb squad, you – infirmary, you – balaclava boys. Blondie, sit by that phone."
The door bangs behind him.

12:27.

The only other phone box is outside the Post Office.

Next to the van.

12:33.

"It's Martha, tell me what's happening…there are still people here, when are you coming?"
"You should have told me a time."
Door open, phone dangling, out in the drizzle, heart pumping, mouth dry.

12:36.

Blank faces, turned backs, heads shaking.
"Run! Go! Get away!"
Tyres splash past, a pram by the van.
Blue flashing lights.

12:42.
Run to the post office, shout at the queue.
"Get out! Now, there's a bomb! Go!"
Back in the rain, grab the pram, push, and run, run, run…leave it round the back of the Post Office.

12:44.

Back to the van, baby's mother grabs him, yell in her face "Round the back!
Run!"
Wrench the van door, engine roars, blue lights through the tears and the rain.
"So sorry, so sorry…"
The van lurches a few yards, then …

12:45.

Double Cross
Rita Stephens

Chrissy hadn't planned to be in Seville at Easter, and yet here she was standing on a balcony high up on the fourth floor of the Hotel Santos. Below, was a throng of people pressed tightly against buildings, creating a human route for the swaying platforms; platforms carrying the life size portrayal of the passion of Christ.

The churches of Seville competed with one another to create the most elaborate depictions of piety, with religious statues in hand carved wood adorned with sumptuous velvets and twinkling gemstones. Incense wafted up to the balcony, just as the thrum of the drum with its regular beat evoked a feeling of guilt in any a lapsed Catholic. She knew that below each swaying platform there were many men shouldering this mighty spectacle of religious fervour, their role unseen behind draped curtains that touched the floor. It was the penitents that guided their way. Hooded and robed with only eye slits in their capirotes, high conical headgear, they guided the platform with flickering candles. The noise was deafening, with drums, music and the gasps of the throng creating a heady mix that tried to ground her to the spot, but she had work to do.

Reluctantly, Chrissy left the sanctuary of the hotel, taking the rear exit that led her along a labyrinth of narrow streets that was, thankfully, both quieter and cool. She knew the geography of Seville well. After a fine arts degree in London, she had specialised in religious antiquities and had spent a year in Seville, studying under the tutelage of one of the finest procurers of museum artefacts, and many summers thereafter, studying the religious treasures that Spain had to offer.

This was the reason she found herself here in Seville; her company, 'Samsonite Antiquities,' had been approached by a client to procure a religious pendant that he wanted to give to his wife. On first meeting her client, Chrissy had felt some misgivings, but put this discomfort down to her own prejudices.

"I want you to go to Seville and purchase a little something for the wife." His heavy jowls seemed to have a life of their own as he looked intently at her. "It's a popery type thing," he had coughed as if cleansing the stain of Catholicism from his mouth.

"She's from Poland." He flipped open his wallet pointing a meaty finger at a picture of a beautiful blonde decades younger than him. "And they're all Catholics there," he snarled. She thought this unlikely but chose not to comment. By now, Chrissy was feeling uncomfortable in the overheated room, with her senses bombarded with the overwhelming smell of aftershave that clung to a man cleavage of curly grey hair. She forced herself to sit upright – after all, she couldn't afford to pick and choose her clients.

"I want you to authenticate the pendant, then phone me and I will do a bank transfer. I have all the paperwork of the provenance of the piece, so if you could look over those I would be most grateful. There'll be a nice little earner in it for you, a top-class hotel and flights." He winked as if there was something seedy about it.

On arriving in Seville, she still had her misgivings; was the information garnered from her client accurate and why had his instructions now led her to the seediest part of Seville? The house, just off the Plaza del Sanchez, like many in this area, must have once been an architectural wonder in its time, but now most of the geometric tiles that had clad the building were either cracked or absent, its present state being no more than a shadow of its former grandeur.

She phoned as instructed. "Am I speaking to Diego Perez?" No answer was forthcoming, but the door was thrown open and an elderly woman, dressed all in black, had beckoned her inside. The room she was led into was sparse of furniture excepting for a dark wooden table, heavily stained and with chairs either end. Sitting in one chair was a man, bloodless, emaciated and yet with eyes that twinkled in greeting, beckoning her to sit.

Little was said before he slid over an encrusted muslin cloth, so dirty that she was fearful of touching it. The woman had joined the man, standing at his shoulder while Chrissy slipped on muslin gloves and took out the tools of her trade. Her anticipation heightened and she took a few calming breaths, carefully unfolding the cloth. She was not to be disappointed. In the 16th century, ten pendants had been made depicting the Virgin Mary and child. The first pendant to be made, the master, had Mary clad in a red robe with a ruby embedded in the mantle, and clusters of diamonds placed around the cross with gold undulations at the edges.

This she knew was securely held in the vaults of the museum and brought out during Lent. Of the nine others that had followed the original, the robe was blue, and each one had been encrusted in smaller diamonds. The jeweller had given those to his daughters, his wife and mother. She knew where eight of those were, spread across the globe in the keeping of people wealthy enough to have purchased them. However, the ninth had never been put up for sale until now. There was no doubt about its authenticity; she had been gifted the chance to study each one, taking her across the globe, appreciating the opportunity to study each one in minute detail.

Chrissy nodded to the couple and said, "I will phone my client. If you will excuse me, it should not take too long. I think the signal is much better outside. If you could bear with me."

A cool breeze met her as she slipped outside and approached the Plaza de Sanchez to make her call. It was a clipped conversation, ending with her client stating, "I will make the transfer now." She returned and nodded to the man, who then left the room, coming back after a few minutes to say that the transfer had successfully gone through. She slipped the pendant into the special case she had brought, shook hands, and left.

She didn't dwell in Seville. She had got what she had come for and the main aim now was to get this very precious icon back and locked in a safe place before handing it over to her client.

Rising from an early call by the hotel staff, a waiting taxi had whisked her to the airport, and it was as she was reading the departure board that the unexpected happened. A male and female police officer approached her. They took her by the elbows and gently but firmly led her into an office. They were pleasant but firm, requesting that she hand over the pendant that they believed was in her possession. Their only reason given for her apprehension was that the pendant would be investigated as possible cultural appropriation, and that if the pendant had left the country, she would be liable for criminal charges.

As Chrissy was later to explain to her client, the only course of action she felt that she had was to hand over the pendant there and then, insisting on a receipt and contact details. She was then marched to the departure lounge and passed through security.

The flight home had given Chrissy too much time to think, with her heart skipping a beat every time she rehearsed what she was going to say to her client. On arrival, she switched off her flight mode and phoned him with some urgency, only to find herself stuttering and stammering over the enormity of the news. He rang off by saying leave it with me.
Two weeks elapsed, two weeks of sleepless nights and heart stopping anxiety, before Chrissy got a call from her client.

"Come round, I've got something to show you." His smarmy voice rather irked her, but she had to know what he had to say. Up to now, no-one in the antiquities' world had got a sniff of this catastrophe, as she saw it, and that was the way she wanted to keep it; her credibility kept the business profitable, and this cock-up was sure to derail it fast.

He had met her as the car swung onto the drive, barely waiting for Chrissy to alight. Rubbing his hands in glee, he couldn't wait to say that "I've got something that will make those pearly whites shine," as he led her into the lounge. "Authenticate that if you will."

"How did you acquire it?" she asked now, clutching the very pendant that she had authenticated in Seville.

"I got a few of my mates from the Costa Del Sol to make a visit. That Perez chap was running a little scam with his family members. A couple of fake police uniforms and a back hander to security at the airport made them think they could get one over me. No bloody way," he spat, "they better be thankful that I only sent Grinder and Chirper to sort them out. Perez and co. were squealing like a babies before they left."

Chrissy left, vowing not to do business with him again.

Humour

The Garden Party
By Daven Potter

Despite the log fire, the drawing room in Maudling Manor carried a distinct midwinter chill as Sir Crispin Crichton sat nursing his brandy and brooded. It was the ingratitude that stuck in his craw. Rather like cook's fondant fancies, but at least they had the decency to melt away. Eventually.

"So remind me," he said. "How long have I been the MP for this damned constituency?"

Lady Margery, with a large blanket wrapped around her knees, sighed but didn't look up from her needlework.

"You know very well you were first elected in 1906 and have now been MP for Much Maudling in the Marsh for 19 years," she said. "And please don't swear, dear."

"Exactly my point. For nearly 20 years I've done my best for the little people who live here - even the horrible socialists who didn't vote for me. In that time I've donated a small fortune to the Party and faithfully supported the Leader through thick and thin."

"I know dear," said Lady Margery. The topic was familiar; her responses well-rehearsed.

"And once more a New Year's Honours list has been published and once more my name's not on it. It's just not good enough."

"No, dear."

"What's wrong with them? Is my money not good enough for them?"

"Don't forget your record of public service, dear. That's what the

Honours system is all about it, isn't it?"

"Yes, of course. Goes without saying," he said.

Lady Margery was waiting. Usually at this point in the conversation her husband liked to remind her that his ancestors had lived at the Manor for the past six generations and every one of his male forebears had been Much Maudling's MP in their turn. But despite this record, not one had risen in rank above that of a 'Knight of the Shire.' Now in his mid-50s, with thinning hair that was already turning white, Sir Crispin felt this was a disgraceful oversight on the part of His Majesty's Government. It was time to put matters right. It was time he was elevated to the peerage. And soon.

Despite Lady Margery's expectations, Sir Crispin surprisingly deviated from his usual script. He rose from his leather wing-backed chair and stood in front of the fire, warming his generous backside. Lady Margery hoped he would move soon and stop blocking what little heat was being given out. Either that or feed the meagre flames with another log. He did neither. Instead he made a declaration.

"I've had an idea," he said. "I've been taken for granted. So I need to do something to remind Prime Minster Baldwin and all the other grandees that I still exist."

"How are you going to do that?" asked Lady Margery, a note of alarm creeping into her voice.

"I propose to hold a garden party in the Manor grounds on Midsummer's Day, followed by a ball in the evening. It will be the finest social occasion the county's seen for years."

Lady Margery put down her needlework and frowned. "Wouldn't it be better to organise something for the ordinary folk, especially with so much poverty and unemployment about?"

Sir Crispin's face turned puce. "Good God woman, are you mad? I don't want the hoi polloi traipsing all over our lawns. It's bad enough the Government has now agreed to pay them an old age pension."

Lady Margery protested, but Sir Crispin couldn't be swayed. Worse was to follow when he told her that organising such an event was beyond her limited abilities. A grand occasion like this had to be planned by a professional. She swallowed the insult along with her pride. Not for the first time.

"By whom?" she asked tersely.

"I thought I would get young Hancox, my secretary, to do it."

Lady Margery inwardly groaned. The man was an utter nincompoop, who was incapable of getting anything right. But her protestations were in vain and the appointment of Hancox prevailed. However, one of her ideas was enthusiastically adopted by Sir Crispin when she suggested holding it in honour of the Prince of Wales's forthcoming trip to southern Africa. And so Hancox was put to work on organising Sir Crispin's 'Grand Celebration of the Royal Tour,' honouring Africa's place in the British Empire.

By the time Spring arrived, preparations were well underway and a meeting took place between Sir Crispin and Hancox to review progress. Sir Crispin was pleased to see that the marquees had been booked and additional gardeners hired to ensure the grounds looked immaculate. Outside catering staff had been employed to help prepare the food, while Sir Crispin's vintners had been consulted about the wines and other drinks required. The musical entertainment had also been thought of with a chamber orchestra engaged, as well as a jazz band to entertain those bright young things who were also expected to attend. And in a further nod to the African theme the staff and servants would be dressed in safari-style uniforms. The highlight, though, was set to be a cavalcade of tableaux, each one representing one of Britain's African colonies.

"It's going to be spectacular," said Sir Crispin. "But what about the guest list?"

"Everyone you and her ladyship instructed me to contact has now received an invitation. I can't think the county will have ever seen such a magnificent occasion," said Hancox with a beaming smile.

Sir Crispin took the list from Hancox and quickly ran his eyes down the names, anxious to make sure Hancox had not omitted anyone of importance from the county set. But as far as he could see, they were all there – the Lord Lieutenant and his wife, the Farquharsons, Forbes, Lyons, Cholmondleys, Urquharts, Bagehots and Buccleughs. He was about to bring the meeting to a satisfactory conclusion when he had a sudden thought.

"I know what's missing," he said. "We need more elephants."

"Are you sure, sir?" asked Hancox with a frown.

"Of course, man! We can't have an event like this without them. See to it," said Sir Crispin.

Hancox was stumped. For the next couple of days he pondered how to satisfy this last minute request from his employer. And then he remembered that one of his old school chums had taken up a new position with London Zoo. After a pleading telephone call to Charles Petty-Fitzwilliam, he was put in touch with a fellow who owned a travelling circus. Even better, the chap was a South African. How appropriate.

Midsummer Day was blessed with glorious weather. The sun shone from an almost cloudless sky and the grounds shimmered immaculately. The air crackled with expectation as Sir Crispin and Lady Margery prepared to welcome their esteemed guests.

"Hancox has excelled himself," said Sir Crispin to his wife an hour later as they stood at the top of the drive, greeting the late arrivals.

"I must admit I'm pleasantly surprised," admitted Lady Margery, looking around. "Where is he?"

"He's in my study attending to one or two other business matters. I'll go and get him while you hold the fort."

As he expected, Sir Crispin found Hancox in the study, working on a couple of legal issues. "Come on, man," said Sir Crispin, "you can deal with that later. You're missing out on all the fun."

"Thank you, sir," said Hancox, closing a manilla folder. He was grateful for Sir Crispin's intervention. The garden party was in full swing and he felt he deserved a drink to celebrate his masterful organisational skills. But as the two men reached the Manor's front entrance they heard a terrible commotion. The music had come to an abrupt and discordant finish, drowned out by a cacophonous trumpeting sound. At the same time they felt the ground tremble beneath them, followed by loud screams and yells, and the sight of 200 people running for their lives across the lawns. The more fleet-footed were heading for the house, while others were climbing trees, jumping into the river and some were hiding in the coronation maze. A group of elderly and infirm guests, led by the Rector, had simply fallen to their knees in prayer.

"What in God's name is going on!" yelled a distraught Sir Crispin.

"I fear it's the elephants," said Hancox. "They must be stampeding."

"What are you on about? What elephants?" demanded Sir Crispin.
"The ones you told me to hire, sir. You said 'we need more elephants'."
Sir Crispin punched Hancox on the shoulder. Hard. "Not elephants, you

blithering idiot! I said 'we need more Oliphants.' It was all very well inviting the Lord Lieutenant, Sir George and Lady Oliphant, but we'd forgotten to invite his two brothers as well."

In despair, Sir Crispin held his head in his hands. "Can it get any worse?" he moaned as Lady Cynthia Oliphant ran past shrieking, with the tattered remnants of her dress hanging off her bloodied back.

Hancox backed away. "So when you said 'we also need more Lyons...'"

Green With Envy
John Welford

My neighbour's lawn's a vibrant green

A finer sward could not be seen.

You never saw such luscious grass,

But he can stick it - let that pass.

My own backyard is wan and pale

As he reminds me without fail:

"Call that a lawn?" he vilely mocks.

I've had it with his verbal knocks.

I'll have to see what I can do

To take him down a peg or two.

Brown dog-pee patches - fearsome sight -

I'm taking Fido round at night.

I'll switch the cans inside his shed

He'll spray with lemonade instead.

And while I'm there, to sink still lower,

Maybe I'll sabotage his mower.

I'll creep around and empty packets

Of lots of lovely leatherjackets.

A lawn looks best with hills and holes

I'll introduce some friendly moles.

What grass hates most, so I've been told,

Is various kind of fungal mould,

So that's my cue, I think I'm right,

To find the most pernicious blight

That makes his pasture lose its hair

Ending up with patches bare.

And when I'm sure his number's up

I'll seed with creeping buttercup.

I wonder, though, perhaps you'll spot

The downside of my fiendish plot?

His lawn is trashed and I have won

The green grass prize, so all is done,

But there's this nagging fear that he

Will come and do the same to me.

Lord Harmington-Booth's Satisfaction

Brent Kelly

Wednesday 11th September 1830 - Grosvenor Square London:

James Parker was finding sleep somewhat elusive and last night had proved no different. He would not however be contacting his medical consultant. The cause of his insomnia was only too evident, something was busying his mind. And until he received news (good or bad) his restless nights would be sure to prosper.

He sat at the window watching as the Square began to come to life. On the table at his side two lightly poached kippers, butter running off onto the plate, waited untouched. It wasn't just sleep deprivation he was suffering from.

A flash of red uniform at his front entrance followed by Hasting's confident steps to retrieve the post-delivery caused the usual flutter in his stomach. For almost a week now the sight of a 'robin' at his door had filled him with a fluttering he was unable to quell. Would today bring the news?

The double doors of the breakfast room as usual opened without a knock. His man entered carrying a silver tray bearing a single letter.

"Your correspondence sir," said Hastings his lips barely moving, "would you have me read it to you?" He asked grudgingly.

James nodded. But knew already what the missive would contain.

"It is from his Lordship, Harmington-Booth and," Hastings paused, his supercilious air momentarily shaken, "it appears that his Lordship is asking for satisfaction. Has something arisen I am unaware of sir?"

"There was an altercation in Blake's last week that I hoped had blown over. Admittedly Hamby had blustered on about having his satisfaction after he accused me of insulting his beloved sister."

"Sir, he is adamant in this letter that he will have his satisfaction at daybreak on Chorley Heath this coming Friday. His choice of weapon is pistols."

Tuesday 3rd September 1830 - Blake's Gentleman's Club:

The club was unusually busy for a Tuesday, but James and Hamby had still acquired the best table in the building for their weekly lunch together. The food arrived quickly and soon they were fulfilled and relaxed enjoying their cigars.

"So, when are you going to do the decent thing by Daphne then hey? She will be four and twenty this coming winter."

There had been much ongoing speculation in society circles that Lord Harmington-Booth had proffered his sister Daphne's hand to his best friend the honourable James Parker. The betrothal however had yet to be formally announced.

It was then James had tentatively broached the fact he had met someone else. Hamby had exploded. The table and its contents were upended and his Lordship had swung for James in blind fury. The members watched on in a shocked silence.

Friday 13th September 1830 - Chorley Heath:

The ornamental silk lined box containing the ancient duelling pistols was placed open on a tree stump. The morning was unseasonably cold and James had seen no one. This was fortunate as duelling, even among the nobility, was now frowned upon in modern society and could have legal ramifications.

"Ah Parker, you have shown your face then. Measly face that it is."

James said nothing, not trusting his voice with the nervous energy coursing through his veins.

"Will you be duelling yourself Parker, or nominating?"

"Nominating."

"And who is to be the lucky man defending your honour?"

"I nominate Hastings," said James and turned to see his man's face fold in horror as he looked across to his Lordship standing next to his nominated man, Truelove, once the best shot in the Coldstream Guards.

Sunday 1st September 1830 - Mansion Place London:

James was feeling somewhat tetchy. "What can a man do Hamby, when they have allowed themselves to be domineered year on year by a bladdy servant of all people?"

"Well my sister's dirty deed, saying she'll never marry you or anyone else for that matter, may give us a little chink of opportunity. I think that the time may have arrived for me to have my satisfaction."

Strange Dream
Phil Whitmore

The other night I had
the straaangest of straaange dreams.
I dreamt I was a dad,
but not by natural means.
Because the baby wasn't born
it was created in my lab.
I decided to call him Shaun,
and Shaun called me a cab.
Because Shaun wasn't human
he wasn't even animal,
he was to be a giant, blooming,
Veggie eating cannibal.
So, Shaun the veggie plant beast
came to live in my old house.
Every day and night he'd like to feast,
but I really mustn't grouse.
Cos I've just won the lotto.
Tens of millions of quids
I went out to get blotto.
Is my life now on the skids?
The day I got arrested,
charged then with drink and driving,
was very much the bestest
day there possibly could be.
Veggie Shaun is on the rampage
destroying half the town.
But I'm locked in my cage
away from any kind of clown.
Coulrophobia is my biggest fear
did I forget to tell you that?
Veggie Shaun, I've brought him here
to rid the world of pratts. [PS Coulrophobia is a fear of clowns.]

It's Not Over Yet!
Rita Stephens

I was surprised to see Ron sitting at our usual table in the snug of the Duck and Partridge; if anyone was early, it tended to be me. We had taken to meeting for a pint and a game of cards once a week ever since Jean, his wife, had died two years ago. We had been a foursome for as many years as I can remember, with Ron, Jean, Marge my wife, and me sharing a meal together, and several long weekends away hiking the by-ways and highways of the countryside. Unfortunately, with the death of Jean, Ron always declined our invitations to join us.

"Sorry mate, you know what they say, two's company… "

I could see that he hadn't noticed me arriving. Being unusually intent on his phone made me a little curious, and I became more so when I looked over his shoulder, catching a fleeting view of a smiling woman being flicked to the left of the screen. I knew what he was up to, but I wasn't going to make it easy for him.

"Hi Ron. What's up, you look as if you're reading bad news?"

He had visibly jumped, swinging round trying at the same time to turn his phone off, which unfortunately fell, forcing me to pick it up, so giving me plenty of time to read, 'It's Not Over Yet, dating agency for the discerning mature.'

If a 68-year-old man could blush, he would have done so; instead, he had rather gruffly grabbed the mobile and said, "What are you having, the usual?" scurrying over to Emma, waiting behind the bar, before returning with two frothy pints and a look that said, 'Mind your own business.' There was no way I was going to do that.

"OK Ron, don't be so high and mighty. I am pleased that you are thinking of joining a dating agency."

For a minute, I thought I had gone too far, as the silence seemed to stretch, and for a short time it was as if we were the only two in the pub.

Then he grinned. "You're right, I have joined. In fact, I took the plunge last week and sent my details in, and I have already had several likes."

"Good for you," I said, taking a large slurp of beer, "what details did you have to give?"

"Well, nothing too onerous, but I did have to give quite a bit of thought to it. I expected them to ask for a photograph, but I was less prepared for the psychobabble stuff... you know, a way of revealing your true self."

"What do you mean, Ron?"

At this, he coughed looking embarrassed. "Well, they asked that if you were a car, what type of car would you be, and then you had to decide on an animal that suited your personality."

"That must have been hard. What car did you go for?"

"Well, that was easy. I just typed in my Bentley, after all it is a vintage model that is still in good nick, so is the quality leather interior, not a mark on it," he said slurping his beer before grinning, "and for an old 'un, it's got plenty of power under the bonnet."

"What! I remember you said that it has been languishing in your garage for six months of the year because it doesn't like the cold. In fact, you said the last time I saw you, that it stutters for ages before it even realises the revs are on."

He looked rather sheepish. "It does need a little warming up, but with the right tinkering it runs smoothly enough if not overused."

It was my turn to stare at him, fighting down the desire to raise my eyes heavenwards.

"OK, don't worry. They won't know your Bentley, and they will probably think of a James Bond type, and he got all the girls. What about the animal. What did you go for?"

"Well, I went for the koala bear because let's face it John, they are cute and cuddly and what woman wouldn't want one sitting on their bed."

I could feel laughter rising to the surface, but I dumbed it down enough to tell Ron, who knows very little about animals, the salient points of the Koala.

"I hope you didn't mention that they sleep at least 20 hours a day, and that they have the smallest brain to body mass." I felt on a roll now.

"Also, they are not social butterflies; in fact, they only spend 15 minutes a day making friends." I then came in with the killer blow. "Did you also know they are also a transmitter of chlamydia?" I felt a bit cruel giving him this fact as I could see him visibly blanch.

"Anyway, don't worry Ron, I am sure your photograph will erase any negativity towards your choices. Which photo did you use?"

He seemed to squirm at this point and mumble, "The one you took on top of Snowdon.'"

"But that was taken 20 years ago."

"Look John, everyone trims off a little of their age. I bet the women do, so my preference was someone between 50 and 60."

"Well, I hope that wherever you meet her, they have a bit of diffused mood lighting, or you might be dumped at the first hurdle," and with that parting shot, I said goodbye.

Four weeks later, John and Marge are celebrating their anniversary at a little Bistro called Mario's.

"Honestly Marge, thank goodness I've got my fire-retardant check shirt on as all these flickering candles makes me very nervous."

"Stop whinging John, we hardly ever go out now. What with you being hard of hearing and your bloody intestinal problems, there's not that many places that cater for grumpy old men."

I thought that that was a bit harsh, especially on our anniversary, but even I had to admit that the flickering flames had brought rather a glow to her face, reminding me why we had lasted 38 years. Just as I was stretching out my hand to stroke hers, we were both startled by raucous laughter coming from the table to the far right. We glanced over, taking in the red upholstered chairs, the seating conveniently placed to provide optimum privacy, for the man anyway, and a rather attractive brunette with what could only be described as a plunging neckline. With every ripple of laughter that emitted from her tiny frame, her breasts seemed to wobble with merriment.

She was oblivious to her surroundings, with all her attention focused on him and, I am ashamed to say, that I rather neglected Marge for the first half hour of our dining. However, I came to my senses when Marge hissed, "I am going to the ladies and I suggest you take your last ogle at that woman's breasts, because when I come back, we are changing seats," and with that she had weaved her way to the back of the bistro, passing the couple in the corner and glancing at the man before disappearing in to the recesses of the women's toilets. When she returned, she had a rather smug look on her face.

"Do you know who is sitting across from that woman?"

I feigned, "What woman?"

She wasn't fooled. "Don't give me that; you have had more interest in her cleavage than you have had for your starters." I was startled to look down and see two stuffed mushrooms nestling in a bed of truffle butter; I hadn't even realised that they had been served.

"Who is it then? Is it someone you know?" I enquired.

"Of course, I know him," she hesitated, "well, I think it's him. You know, your best mate Ron. The person you see every week down at the Duck and Partridge." This bit of information had really taken the wind out of my sails.

"Well why didn't you say hello?"

"Don't be daft John, he didn't clock me, and the way things look I don't think he wants company."

As if on cue, the couple rose and turned, causing me to look at Ron straight in the face.

My goodness! What a transformation. He had obviously abandoned his ubiquitous check shirt for a pink linen one, with a natty leather jacket and chinos completing the ensemble. They were soon strolling over on their way to the exit. They didn't linger. There seemed to be some urgency to get home. He merely smiled, waved, and then winked, putting his hand in the curve of his companion's back before ushering her swiftly past.

"I can't believe that was Ron! You didn't tell me he had got his teeth whitened… and that tousled hair look really suited him. There is certainly life in the old dog yet," she said, looking over at me with a critical eye.

"You'd better up your game," she snarled.

Wild Water
John Welford

My niece and her friends went out for the day -
That's Karen, my dear sister's daughter -
They chose the fast river as somewhere to play
A scheme that just didn't hold water.

Not much long before, in a moment of zeal,
All the parts for a boat I had bought her.
I reckoned she needed a craft with a keel
To set sail on such choppy rough water.

But one of her friends, amazingly daft -
If only our Karen had fought her -
Thought maybe they only needed a raft
To have fun on that turbulent water.

So off they all set, that fine afternoon,
Like lambs to an ultimate slaughter,
They found to their cost, and that pretty soon,
That rafts are no good in rough water.

They should have foreseen, had they had any sense,
And my niece had recalled what I taught her,
That rivers in spate will bite you, and thence
At least one would end up in the water.

The girl who fell in at least didn't drown
It was Karen who reached out and caught her.
They all got ashore and sat themselves down
So glad they'd escaped from the water.

This lesson they learned, the hard way it's true -
Don't do things that you just didn't oughter.
Disaster is what will most likely ensue
When you play with a raft on wild water.

Counting the Cost of Christmas
Daven Potter

Santa had spent the last few days at his North Pole HQ completing his annual audit and the final figures didn't look good. With a sigh, he pushed aside his laptop and turned to his Chief Elf.

"There's no getting away from it, Blinky," he said. "Christmas has become ruinously expensive."

Blinky grimaced. It was the news he was dreading after watching Santa's jovial smile and the twinkle in his eye slowly fade over the course of the last week. What were they going to tell his small army of elves, resplendent in their smart new green and red uniforms, who were happily going about their tasks in the adjoining workshops, oblivious to the financial difficulties?

"What are we going to do, boss?" he asked, his long, pointy ears drooping with dismay.

"There are no easy answers, I'm afraid. The kids of today are no longer satisfied with dolls and Dinky toys. You've seen their wish lists – they want smartphones, VR headsets, e-this and e-that. If it isn't battery-powered, they're not interested."

"Couldn't we economise?" suggested Blinky, scratching his straggly ginger beard.

"Cut back on their presents?" said Santa, his bushy white eyebrows arching to a point where they threatened to merge with his hairline.

"Have you any idea what it's like for a parent to wake up on Christmas morning and witness their child having a tantrum because their present wasn't quite what they wanted? Or someone forgot to include the right battery with it? The kids would never eat their brussels sprouts after a debacle like that. And besides, cutting back would rather negate the whole point of our existence."

"I was thinking more of all those mince pies that Mrs C makes for you. And the sherry."

"Excuse me. What are you suggesting?"

"What I'm suggesting," said Blinky, pointing to Santa's rotund physique in comparison to his own skinny frame, "is that as well as saving money, a diet might have health benefits."

"Go without my mince pies? Forget it," said Santa, rubbing his well-fed stomach. "In any case it would ruin my image as well as my figure."

"Hmm," said Blinky. "Well, what are we going to do, then?"

"Well, I've thought about asking all the elves to work unpaid overtime," said Santa, who held up his hand to quell Blinky's immediate objection, "and I've looked at cutting back on the carrots and apples we give to the reindeer as treats. But both measures would be counterproductive. So there's nothing for it – I'm going to have to bring in an outside investor."

Blinky's brow knotted, as much in suspicion as surprise. "What kind of outside investor?" he asked.

In response, Santa bent down to pick up his briefcase, which was under his desk. He rested it on his knees while he popped open the lid, taking out a sheaf of papers and setting them down on the desktop. He riffled through the documents until he found the one he was looking for.

"Two options. The first is a young American guy called Jerry Swizzel, who's a twenty-something cryptocurrency tycoon," he said, showing Blinky a photo of Jerry Swizzel that he'd paper-clipped to the sheet of paper. "I'm told he's a trillionaire."

"Who told you that?"

"He did."

"Well, there's no arguing with a megalomaniac," said Blinky as he inspected the picture, which showed a young man with electrified hair, messianic eyes and a fierce grin. "Please don't tell me he's also got a 'vision thing'."

"He's certainly got big plans to go with his big hair. He says the brand – that's us, by the way – has a 'mega amount' of untapped potential."

"Let me guess, he wants to 'big up' Mrs C and give the reindeer a higher profile."

Big up? Santa frowned at his assistant's choice of words, vis-a-vis Mrs C. Just because the pair had worked closely together for the last 500 years, was no reason for Blinky to become over-familiar. "Leaving aside your thoughts on my wife – and do please leave them aside – he wants to expand the Elf on the Shelf operation and launch a takeover bid for the Tooth Fairy. He says he'd also like to do something creative with a snowman."

Blinky shook his head. "A snowman? Mark my words, boss, it'll all end in tears," he said. "Or, at the very least, a big puddle on the floor. Has he got any more bright ideas?"

"He's asked me if there are any large lithium deposits under the North Pole that we can mine to make our own batteries."

"Oh boy," said Blinky. "So who's the other option?"

Santa shuffled through his bundle of papers again, before pulling out the one he wanted. "The other choice," he said, "is a middle east country's Sovereign Wealth Fund. It seems they've run out of football clubs to buy and want to move into the children's market."

"So, not so much 'sports washing' as 'kids washing'," said Blinky, sourly.

"Although there's no doubt some of the little blighters could do with a bar of soap, along with their other presents."

Santa stroked his fulsome white beard in contemplation. "Maybe. But something has to be done."

And something was done. After further consideration, Santa decided against the Sovereign Wealth Fund's offer. "They were going to build the world's biggest ice cave in the middle of the desert and relocate us," he told Blinky with a sad shake of his head. "They also wanted to swap the reindeer for camels. But can you imagine all the Christmas cards – they just wouldn't look right with pictures of camels pulling a sand yacht across a snowy landscape. And despite the cave's air conditioning, the chances are it would be far too hot for me to wear my signature red coat, trousers and big black boots. On top of which, I'm too old and set in my ways to start wearing a t-shirt, shorts and flip-flops."

"And too round," said Blinky, who was still agitating for Santa to go on a diet.

Santa, however, ignored the interruption. "So that's mainly why I've sold a majority interest to the American," he said.

"A majority interest. Is that wise?"

"That remains to be seen," said Santa with a wry smile. "Meanwhile, it's time for Jerry to put his bitcoin where his mouth is."

But that's where things went horribly wrong, for Jerry Swizzel turned out not to be as rich as he said he was – or as rich as any of the speculators who frequented the cryptocurrency trading websites thought he was, come to that. Not only were his expansion plans put on ice, so to speak, but he was desperate to make swingeing economies. To that end, he organised a Zoom call from his Malibu beach house to explain his plans to Santa.

"Yo, Beardy," he said, with all the false enthusiasm he could manufacture.

"Hello Jerry," said a wary Santa.

"Mega development on the Christmas Eve delivery front."

"Really?"

"Yeah, I've decided to let you, Rudy and the other guys go. We need to move to a new delivery platform, going forwards. It's an app called Reindr – the kids will love it. It's linked to a fleet of funky red-nosed delivery e-bikes."

Santa sighed. "Not happening," he said, holding up the sales contract.

"What's that?"

"It's the small print, Jerry. Or to be more precise, it's sub section 12, paragraph 35, which refers to all operational changes requiring unanimous agreement."

"So?"

"So it's a veto, Jerry – my very own Santa clause."

Killing Villanelle
Bob Crockett

Poetic assassin sent from hell.

My literary antagonist

You damned infernal villanelle.

You torment my brain and every cell

Though I implore you to desist

Poetic assassin sent from hell.

Oh, exceptionnelle demoiselle

I'll try my best if you insist

You damned infernal villanelle.

My fear of failure I cannot quell

No matter how valiantly I persist

Poetic assassin sent from hell.

But I will storm your citadel

And go enter this one in the list

You damned infernal villanelle.

For I have found 'ma Tourterelle'

And I hope that you will get the gist.

Poetic assassin sent from hell

You damned infernal villanelle.

Top Button

Farren

Oh dear! Oh dear! Oh, dearie me! Do stop crying. You're perfectly safe. And believe me, you've come to a good home.

I know! I know! It may seem dark in here, but you will soon get used to it. How many of you are there? Let's see… one, two, three, four, five, six, seven down the front, eight, nine for the collar, short sleeves so none there… and then, oh yes, a spare inside. You must be good quality if you have a spare, and that logo confirms it. You are attached to a very fine casual shirt.

Me? I'm Top Button in this wardrobe. Not that that implies I'm in charge. Simply I'm the top button on the master's best suit, and my colleagues are Middle and Bottom, plus Inside Pocket, four small ones on each sleeve, (four on a sleeve is also a sign of quality), Spare, inside the jacket, and Back Pocket, on the suit trousers. Altogether there are fourteen of us, all firmly attached.

So, you're all newly unwrapped and all you can remember is the noisy factory and the busy store where you were bought today. I've been here a long time, ten years, but some buttons can be in work for decades.

The first thing you need to know is that you are safe here. Every home has two families, people, who wear the clothes and the button family who are in various places around the house. We're the lucky ones in the wardrobe, regularly going out and performing our jobs. Others in bottom drawers don't get out much. And of course, every house has a button box where some of us will retire to when our clothes are worn out.

That doesn't happen so much these days. People don't wait for clothes to wear out, they just get fed up with them and then either pass them to a charity shop for other people to buy or worst of all, put them in the dustbin for landfill, the ultimate indignity for a button. And they rarely save their buttons because very few can sew or even bother to make repairs to their clothes. However, let me cheer you up. It's a good life here. This family look after their clothes. You will be washed after every wear, and you mustn't be scared of that, and then you will be sent out to be ironed. Suits like us are sent to the dry cleaners. Being sent out is our opportunity to meet buttons from other homes and hear their stories.

Buttons are very good storytellers. When I first came here, a button on an old suit, long since departed, told me about a brass button he'd met, attached to an army uniform belonging to the great grandfather. We think the uniform is still here up in the loft. Anyway, this button had been in use in Normandy on D-Day, and actually survived the war. What a hero!

Then next door in madam's wardrobe is a dress totally covered in buttons, all gold. Apparently, she wore it for a Buckingham Palace Garden Party, but it's never been out since. So, you never know where you may travel to. And it's not hard work. My colleague, Bottom, never has to do anything as it is the fashion to leave the bottom button undone on the suit jacket. He's got royal connections as the fashion commenced in sympathy with the overweight King Edward VII who was obliged to leave his bottom button undone in order to wear his waistcoat and did the same when "casual" suits replaced riding jackets.

You may wonder why buttons on men's clothes are on the right side, whereas ladies' buttons are on the left. The answer is that in olden days this allowed a man's dominant right hand unhindered access to a pistol or a sword. Conversely, ladies buttons went on the left so as to make dressing by a right-handed lady's maid a smoother process. Pistols, swords and lady's maids are long gone but they still sew us buttons in those same places. You have a lot to learn but plenty of time to gossip.

Most buttons like us have a gentle life. Unless, of course, you are unfortunate enough to be attached to the clothes of a gardener, a sportsman, a nurse, a farmer, or other person engaged in strenuous physical activity. Those buttons have a tough time, out in all weathers, stretched to the limit of their strength and in danger of being pulled off, broken, or simply detached. If you are lost on the ground, you will suffer a truly risky adventure into the unknown and I wouldn't give a button for your chances of survival.

Saxon Paddocks
Hugh Tibbits

Saxon Paddocks is an ordinary man; extremely tall but otherwise ordinary; moon-white, unruly hair and beard but otherwise ordinary; born prone to the wildest of mood swings but otherwise an ordinary man. His ordinariness he'd inherited from his mother Vivien, a devotee of calm acceptance, a slight woman, charming in manner with an unrivalled ability to meld into a crowd, merge into the nondescript, an exponent of the sickeningly bland.

They say opposites attract. If Vivien personified commonplaceness then Etruscan Paddocks embodied idiosyncratic eccentricity. He, unlike his son, was petite in stature other than in one particular zonal area of anatomy, he possessed a penchant for excessive drinking and for hell raising melodramatics. He'd acquired a fortune from his late father, Persian, a self-made millionaire who'd amassed a fortune from dabbling (he a renowned dilettante) in other people's businesses.

By the time Saxon came of age, the family fortune had shrivelled, Etruscan having spent every last penny he possessed on a futile quest to perfect the cut of self-fulfilling breeches, frustrated by the lack of choice in a good trouser for the smaller man with extra-large equipment. Saxon had failed to cover himself in glory during his school career, he not naturally bright, had wrestled with ambition, conflicted by the variance of parental expectation, his mother having set her sights on him achieving mediocrity whilst his father had demanded his son attain alpha academic attributions. Predictably he'd failed to meet either requirement, having spent great swathes of lesson-time in the sick bay, pumped full of intravenous anxiolytics by the school nurse in a vain attempt to steady his ambivalence.

Toward the end of Saxon's last term at school, Viv and Etruscan had sat him down for a serious 'heart to heart.' Viv explained to their bewildered son their pecuniary demise, she having handed over the housekeys to Mr

Rusk that morning, the bank calling in the debt accrued against the second mortgage Etruscan had taken out the previous year on Brascote Manor, the palatial family home set in over eight hundred acres of prime South-West Leicestershire pastureland. She explained to the nonplussed teenager that daddy and she were moving to an apartment on the Norfolk coast which only had enough room for the two of them, meaning Saxon, at sixteen was to be left to his own devices.

The last time he saw his parents, on the steps of Brascote Manor, a taxi parked up on the gravel forecourt, the driver impatiently revving the engine of the Hillman Imp, his mother had handed him his Post Office savings book which contained a healthy £108.79, had kissed his forehead as he'd bent to hug her, had promised to write to him once they were settled into the hostel for broken-back gentry in Great Yarmouth. His father nodded toward his son and then they, his animated parents, were gone. Gone for good.

Although he'd officially left the school, the institution turned a blind eye to his continued attendance, ignored the telltale signs of his overnight occupancy of the sick bay, even provided revamped school dinners at weekends and all because Nurse O'Mara had developed a soft spot for the lad. She'd been the one to take him to the Post Office to withdraw his savings, had been the one to launder his boxer shorts, had been the one who'd comforted wretched moments of despair when he'd succumbed to the angst he'd felt, abandoned and incapably alone. And when Ms Wallop-Curtis, Principal, had called time on his extended tenure, it was Nurse O'Mara who'd taken him home to her terraced house on Highfields Road and watered and fed him.

As any good health professional will attest, recovery takes time. Nurse O'Mara placed Saxon in the recovery position and waited for signs of revival. Waited whilst he dabbled in watercolours, waited whilst he reread the classics, waited whilst he slept and bathed, bathed and slept, ate and lounged, lounged and farted. Waited whilst he shed skin, punched the wall, bawled at the moon, experimented with fury.

Watched and waited, waited and watched, smears on the bedsheets, the headboard notched. Waited until waiting had run its course and then she'd sat him down for a serious 'heart to heart.'

"Time for an occupation young man" declared surrogate O'Mara, accompanying Saxon to the careers advisor, a mellow woman, Ms Fairminded. Having skimmed through the brochures he plumped for a career in hairdressing, he instinctively drawn to the cut and thrust of the salon floor. And so it was on a dreary September morning Saxon Paddocks commenced his stylistic odyssey.

'A Cut Above,' owned by Neville and Nigella Nicelydoesit, attracted a mixed demographic of customers, from the well-to-do old dears from Lash Hill to a younger crowd from Queens Park. Neville, a prize winner in his youth, was feisty but fair, Nigella, warm and comforting. At first Saxon swept the floor, made coffee and twiddled his thumbs until one day, high-peaking in mood, he'd demanded "a go with the scissors." Nigella, overcome by his spirited self-advocacy, let him wash the head of one Grace Gorringe, daughter of the Gorringes from Salisbury Drive, a young woman in her early twenties with flair for the undramatic, she reminding Saxon of his mother.

Hair washed, Nigella, in a moment of rash indecision, handed Saxon the scissors and turned her attention to Mrs Lump-Mastiff, a parish councillor from Aston Flamville. Confronted by a head of hair, the young Saxon baulked momentarily until something quite extraordinary occurred; he was overcome by a stream of confidence, his Damascus moment he was later to name it, and he attacked Grace's barnet with unprecedented vigour. She was delighted by the result, no, more than delighted, she was ecstatic. And not only Grace, every man, woman and child in the salon turned to appreciate Saxon's artistry and the rest, as is written in the best and worst of narratives, is history.

Saxon Paddocks is an ordinary man. Excessively tall, unruly haired, moody but ordinary. He still lives in his home town of Hinckley, still goes to work each morning, opening his salon by seven. He still prides himself on his subdued reputation, still visits Nurse O'Mara every Sunday, she now retired with cats and lumbago, for afternoon tea, still accedes to the highs and lows of bipolar extensions yet one would say…. 'all is well.'

He is a self-made man, owner of the largest chain of salons in Western Europe, friseur to the stars, is married to Grace, their children Roman and Tudor happily home-schooled by personal tutors. Once he'd accrued his first million he'd sought out his parents, found them satisfactorily rooted in the good earth of Norfolk, his father under the ground, he dying as a result of premature evacuation, his mother above ground, working as a typist for the milk marketing board. She's now retired and living in the annexe of Saxon and Grace's modest four bedroomed semi on Butt Lane.

Sometimes at night, when the world is at rest, Saxon can be found sat by the French windows overlooking the back garden, his Post Office savings book in hand, his eyes raised to the heavens as he counts his lucky stars.

A Fruity Limerick

Chris Rowe

An aspiring young lady of Hinckley

With plum in her mouth spoke distinc'ly

But alas all too soon,

It turned into a prune

Creating a well-spoken Wrinkly.

Cats
Daven Potter

I never did like cats even when I was a kid. I'm tempted to blame my mother for that, seeing as I've always held Cathy responsible for everything bad that has happened to me.

"Don't touch that cat," she used to say if I ever bent down to stroke one of the neighbour's pets. "It might bite or scratch; or you might catch fleas or rabies and start frothing at the mouth."

Admittedly they were very large, wild-looking creatures, so it was understandable that I grew up with a distrust of the animals. But when did that fear transmogrify into a phobia of anything pertaining to 'cats'? I know the answer without having to think too hard about it: it was when Cathy took me to the doctor's suffering from catarrh when I was five-years-old and I caterwauled for the whole time I was at the GP's surgery.

That was what did it. From then on I was back and forth from the doctor's suffering from a whole catalogue of medical catastrophes. After the catarrh it was cataracts and then there was the time when an exotic Persian cat wafted the fluffiest tail I'd ever seen against my leg and I collapsed in a state of frozen terror. The hospital specialists told me afterwards that it could have been catalepsy, or maybe catatonic schizophrenia, but they weren't too sure because the symptoms are similar and they were reluctant to categorise my condition.

Friends cattily asked me if it was catching and I categorically assured them it wasn't. I was sent to see psychiatrists, psychologists and hypnotherapists, as well as neurologists, serologists and even an immunologist, who thought I might have a catabolism.

"A what?" I asked him and was preparing to demand a CAT scan until he reassured me that he was simply referring to a possible problem with my metabolism. Except a blood test came back clear and I was close to despair because none of these medical experts had the answer.

And then I went on a writers' course and the experience proved cathartic because I met a tutor there and she instantly diagnosed my problem.

"I've seen this once before with a Booker Prize reject," she said. "It's called catachresis."

I looked at her blankly and checked to see if I felt faint or even more abnormal than usual before daring to ask about my prognosis.

"It's nothing to worry about," she said, "unless you're planning a career as a professional writer. In which case your misuse or strained use of words, occurring either in error or for rhetorical effect, may prove catastrophic."

Tragedy in SW19
John Welford

She sat in her chair, halfway to the sky
To watch whatever the players let fly -
She came every year, this place and this time
And issued her judgments when seated on high.

She watched with keen eye the battlers in white -
No better view, this empyrean height -
No error escaped her gimlet-like gaze
As she swivelled her head both leftwards and right.

When perched in her seat, her word was the law.
She opened her mouth - a bellowing roar
Let all present know how everything stood -
She said what was what and shouted the score.

You had to obey. A choice there was none
As squaddies would know, careers just begun -
A stern sergeant-major away from the chair -
Both of her functions, she did them for fun.

Twas hard to credit the size of her trap:
A cavernous space, voluminous gap
Appeared whenever she unclenched her jaw -
That was the cause of the dreadful mishap.

The match, a stunner, proceeded at pace
As pass followed pass and ace followed ace.
The crowd was entranced, they cheered and they whooped
The final was next - who would win the place?

A closely matched pair, they fought tooth and nail
Giving their all for this sport's holy grail.

They had been there for hours, two sets apiece,
No way of telling which one would prevail.

But then something happened that silenced the mob
A shot went astray, a badly aimed lob,
Our umpire looked up to follow its flight
But guess where it landed? Plumb in her gob.

No doubt about it – the ball was stuck fast
The cheers died at once, all there were aghast.
Grim wheezes and croaks were all one could hear
Clearly this lady would soon breathe her last.

Her face turned a vile and rare shade of puce
They tried to revive her, twas not any use -
Brought down from her chair, no more could she speak
Save one final thing and that word was "Deuce!"

Where There's a Will
Farren

"Look here my friend, you say you're a bard… OK, you say you're The Bard, but to me you're nothing but trouble. You come into my pub spouting a few rhymes and expecting me to give you free ale. I'm a businessman, an 'ardworking one, opening all hours God sends, and for what? So that you and your mates can come in 'ere out of the cold to sit in comfort on my chairs in front of my fire, poking the logs paid for by me, and expecting free ale? You must be joking!

You are joking, because my customers do not want to hear your boring, ramblin,' never ending verses of merry widows, foreign gentlemen and fairies in a wood. They come here for peace and quiet, a chance to sit and quench their thirst after a hard day's graft. And who wants to be reminded of battles and witches and 'unchbacks? No-one in this village.

… You've got skills have you? What skills? Any that count in earning a living? Have you ever done a proper day's work in your life? I can rhyme, anyone can rhyme.

Listen.

If you come in my pub
You must pay for your grub.
And the ale is not free.
No! Not even for thee
You don't get owt for nowt.
So go get yourself out
Work darn hard for a crust
Only then if you must
Come back in with a coin.
And these drinkers you'll join.
There mate. Made up, just like that. Now bugger off."

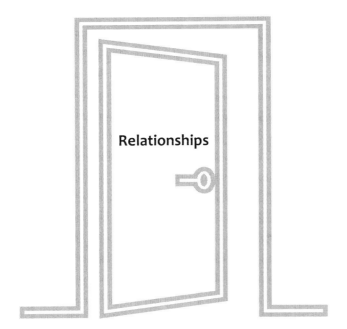

Relationships

Lives Misleading Signposts
Sylvia J. Turner

She floated like an elegant swan.
Hilda was beautiful and serene,
in her early bloom of womanhood,
and the happiest she'd ever been.
Hilda was quite the perfect angel,
and was as pure as the driven snow,
ready to marry and settle down,
with the handsome man she'd got to know.
The prettiest girl in the village,
deeply in love with Franz her beau,
life without him, she'd never envisage,
as she readied her wedding trousseau.
A mass wedding for the local pairs,
was planned for the Harvest Home,
her future all mapped out, free from cares
she thought she would never be alone.
Signs posted for the throng's arrival,
vital guests were on their way,
to enjoy the eve of Harvest Festival,
making merry for the weddings the next day.
Franz's gaze wondered to a pretty girl's guise,
on a balcony, reading a book.
Her beautiful smile and fluttering eyes,
caught him like a fish on a hook.
Lured to the trap of forbidden fruit,
t'would lead him quite astray,
with no thought of his darling, Hilda,
or their cherished wedding day.
Hilda had spotted that look on his face,
his attraction, to the mystery girl,
Hilda followed him to a strange, dark place
her head was in a total whirl.

The sign read 'Dr Coppelius'
the crazy old mad professor,
his inventions were weird and copious.
rooms overflowing with toys he'd treasure.

His skills mixed wizardry, alchemy and mania,
in each life-size mechanical toy,
the girl with the book, he called 'Coppelia,'
she was the professor's pride and joy.
He treated her like a 'daughter,'
and wanted her to be alive.
So, he hatched a plan for slaughter,
a wicked thing to contrive.

He needed a young heart and soul to transplant,
into his 'daughter's' persona,
to bring her to life! what an evil slant,
and young Franz was the perfect donor.
Hilda was hiding as a doll, whilst his evil plot played out,
then the doctor drugged her darling Franz.
He was about to kill him. She had no doubt,
distraction was needed, a doll like dance.
She had to take her chance.

Just in time she dragged poor Franz away,
escaped the terror of the doctor's claws.
Franz saw the error of his ways, some would say,
steering clear of temptations lustful jaws.
But who can really read all the 'signs,'
without misreading the misleading
and keep between those straight and narrow lines
when 'Signs' 'can' be quite deceiving?

Terror can Taste so Sweet

Rita Wilson

"Jump" the Boss orders, "Jump!"

I hover on the edge of the wall behind the toilet block where we are not supposed to play.

"Alien is a sissy, Alien is a sissy," chant the rest of the gang making spooky shapes with their arms and bodies as they creep along the bottom of the wall.

Alien is my nickname due to the fact one of my eyes is a green blue, the other green brown, hazel. My grandma says it is because I am special but I do not feel special perched on the edge of this wall, my whole body trembling.

"Jump!" demands the Boss. He is stationary, staring up at me with a menacing look in his eyes. He is the undisputed Boss of out motley gang of eleven-year-olds. We all did whatever he commanded or suffered the consequences.

Taking a deep breath I jump. As my breath escapes rapidly I cry out in pain. My right leg is at an odd angle under my body. The gang scarper as soon as I land on the concrete.

The teacher on duty hears my screams and there is a huge commotion as play-time is cut short. Being the last day of term it is supposed to be an extra-long one. The sirens of a distant ambulance can be heard and all goes quiet and it gets nearer to the school. On the way to the hospital I think will I be able to ride my bike again. Run races? Play football?

It all happened a long time ago and the worst part of it was missing out on a whole summer as my leg healed. By the time I was up and doing the things I might never do again it was September and the gang had dispersed to different comprehensive schools. My parents had chosen a grammar school for me in an effort to separate me from the gang. The wonderful treatment that I received at the hospital had a lasting effect on me and I am fairly certain that is why I chose to enter the medical profession.

After years of studying, training at medical school, surgery residency, I returned to my home town for a position in the A and E department. It is only occasionally, when I catch sight of my right knee that I am reminded of that summer and what started my successful career off. Until today.

News has come in of two cars colliding in the town centre. Not exactly an emergency situation but one of the drivers has a chunk of shattered windscreen lodged in his forehead.

Scrubbed up ready to perform the surgery to remove it, I note the name on the patient's chart. Frank Finnemore. It is not a name that I would easily forget even after all these years. Frank is wheeled into the operating theatre. I give a quick rundown of the surgery I will be performing and ask "Any questions?"

"Will there be a scar?" he wants to know.

"Well now then Boss," I reply with a huge emphasis on Boss and trying to put a menacing look on my face. "That depends on whether my knife slips or not."

I have been told that the bright lights in the operating theatre emphasise the different colours in my eyes. Frank looks above my mask into my eyes to see if I am joking. I hear a gasp.

I nod to the anaesthetist, poised ready, and within seconds Frank is lying motionless on the operating table but not before a look of sheer terror has brought a sweet taste to my mouth.

Love Her

Simon Rees-Jones

When the world is just noise
– and no sense at all.
Hear her.

If nobody listens
– you need to be heard.
Tell her.

Everything's ugly
– you think there's no grace.
Watch her.

Life is cold, even hard
– no comfort, no warmth.
Hold her.

Because she can teach you
to know how to live.
Love her.

Don Quixote and the Mermaid
Hugh Tibbits

Connections are complex chains.
Dredge the synapses;
spark to life. Reminders.
I am drawn to you like flight to flame,
Like bared soul to honeyed ledge.
Drawn like filings to magnetic frame
like crass lemmings toward the ravine edge.

Are you drawn to dissonance,
is there something in your past that resonates
with the trails I've wandered,
with dreams I've sown,
with songs I've stolen from broken bards,
with soundwaves that sail distance, ocean wide and fearless?

A widened lake where sun, skinny dipping, dives. An unremitting phrase
to etch the soul, to narrow heart, that promotes uncharacteristic charm,
flooding the senses into submission. I caught your eye across the room,
fell into you. And ever since I have been on an endless quest to
reconnect with separation. The fragment you left me, a precious
eucharist, a mirror to my soul, like an expansive exultant epiphany.

Ridiculed - they laughed at my sad countenance, those who bootlegged
love, who scoffed at my attempts at intimacy, fearing they'd be left high
and dry. They paraded me in front of judgement seat, cobwebbed and
skeletal, accused me of plagiarism of the heart, accused me of wretched
deceit; fingers pointed at charts and graphs to illustrate my expansive
insanity.

'He makes much from a mountainous nothing, pretends she stole his
affection in a fleeting moment, an altercation with destiny. Name her or
provide us with a photofit description, produce her here in this court. But

you cannot sir, can you? For She is but a figment of your imagination.'

For a brief moment I am stumped, hurtled into doubting my own
certainty, feared I may have caught your glimpse from daydreams,
feared I may have concocted your memory from longing, may have
incited imagination to produce your being in my mind's eye. But it is then
I hear it, the phrase, and you flood back into me like an eagerness, a rip
tide of consequence, course through me like fire,
light me like a northern dance,
radiate my doubt with uncompromising brightness
and you are back, my passenger of light.
I carry you in a forever space, sacred, holy, fertile.

I stand condemned by small grey men with nothing to show for life but
weasel breath. I am care-less in their presence, they can lead me from
their dock, haul me to their Calvary,
hang me from their tree,
I care not, for you are and always will be within; wholly me.
Connections are forged by the merest sleight of a wind, a wisp of
circumstance. Fate or divination, loaded dice or unerring sacrifice?

I sat to one side, you to the other, paired by the briefest of glances. A
short time spent in company, a seduction of soul. I have no recollection
of the words we spoke, no images to conjure, no scents to instigate
tangible memory. I possess only the sense of you, the quiver, the rustle
you evoked, evoke, you disappeared inside me, home, nested; at rest.

And I have not suspended you in place or time. You have no substance,
no form. Not that you are a notion, no far from it, you are life itself.
Without you I would crumple, fall, a pile of broken bones, a skin, a sack.

You are
pulse
beat
flow.

Dulcinea. There, I name her. Princess of my realm. Born not to riches but raised in virtue, born to frequent air and water, to lull the angry-headed beasts of dawn. Her poverty is her fortune, her beauty her recompense. Her dulcet tones ring out as she sings to the soft pluck of dulcimer, the stars dulled by her radiance; dual lights are we to barren skies.

My quest, my quiet odyssey through life, bland yet bejewelled by her opulent grace, is made rarer still by my knowing she journeys too, a quiet lap, she born in me, me in her; to reunite at a given point when we will consummate our love; at journey's end, when all will be revealed, when love will be permitted full voice to recite our proclamations. Will someone record our words for prosperity's sake, a living proof that I speak the truth? Love exists unfettered.

Can love ever be called unrequited? Does such sweetness deserve such bitter rancour? Does she not hold the glimpse of me as dear as I hold mine of her, our tenuous moment forged of a sterner steel, a fabric, fire tested and proven. For is not fledgling love unspoilt by the burden of proof, unsullied by tired parody, clean of the dirt thrown as love spirals, unmasked and commonplace. Is fledgling love not ever ready to fulfil the promise of virgin wings, untainted by the hackneyed flights of fancy?

Our brief encounter inspired lifelong pursuit; chase the dragon. You are in my veins, my first hit, high, hallucinations of a different world, a kinder space. You in your watery depths, me with my uncertainty, you with your dip and dive, me with my trusty steed.

Are you my madness, my rearguard action, my thick headedness, my dalliance?
I answer my own call.
You are not my madness. You are my humble gift, real as any wish I might ever cast, a longing watered place.
Summoned by the phrase, the sparsity of notes on stave, you are my anthem to veracity, my drumroll, my patterned eve, my silver flute.

When life comes to part my way, when my tired eyes fade,
within the mystery of dying moments,
when I at last lay down my lance and shield,
when sun dips to mark my curtain call, there and then I will once more
stand upon your shore and watch as you grasp the air and rise from the
depths, accomplished.

Anthem:

Deeper still this night hangs long on dreams we dared to banish.
Measure for measure the rolling throng wave on wave rising to vanish.
Into the vastness the darkest unknown
hung up on uniqueness that keeps us alone.
Still hoping for angels who might guide us home
yet knowing that the journey is walked on your own.

Refrain:
I was out tilting at windmills
a broken sword clenched in my hand.
And you were out dancing with dolphins
unable to reach dry land.

Further down familiar roads where feet tread different beats.
Distance seems to know no bounds weaving loss between the sheets.
Toward tomorrow's ship with no name,
hung up on the ritual that confuses the game.
I'm nobody's hero with dragons yet slain
guilt like some anchor goes slipping its chain.

Refrain:
I was out tilting at windmills
a broken sword clenched in my hand.
And you were out dancing with dolphins
unable to reach dry land.

Protecting hearts from sorrow's gain my words get caught up in chances.
Shadows dart and find their mark as a lowly mermaid dances.
I stood at the edge to challenge their myths
you rose from the water like some bearer of gifts.
I waited for you to disappear like the mists
but you stood there triumphantly unclenching your fists

Refrain:
I was out tilting at windmills
a broken sword clenched in my hand.
And you were out dancing with dolphins
unable to reach dry land.

The Breakup

Cindie Hall

The last thing she said
filled me with dread:

She needed her own place
and much more space.

Never having peace
always feeling unease.

Looking out for herself
to protect her mental health.

The ties did sever
we were not meant to be together.

We'd been here before
I knew this for sure.

But now miles apart
it broke my heart.

I thought we knew the score
I wanted much more.

But now in my past
it wasn't meant to last.

I had to go onto a new life
and how sad she'll never now
become my wife.

The Last Resolution [The Big One]

Sylvia J. Turner

It was early spring. Time to make some concrete plans for the summer. The last year had flown by, every year whizzing by, faster than the last. Jackie's list of New Year's Resolutions was pretty much resolved apart from one. The one she really should have faced up to. The Big One! The one she had held over from previous years.

For most of her adult life, she had been made aware that she could access records relating to her birth, but she was happy with herself in her adopted alter ego. She had been adopted at birth by her adoring family and now at 25, contemplating the future and settling down, she decided it was time to find out who her birth mother really was. All she had been told was that her mother was a young student who died.

Now armed with some new information, was it the time to seek the links to her blood relatives and genetic heritage, or would it ruin everything? The adoption papers were placed in front of her in a manila file. They showed the name the midwives had given to her 'Jacqueline Isaacs' and the name of her adoptive parents. When she turned to the death certificate it showed her mother's name was 'Sarah,' a Jewish name meaning 'princess.' She immediately loved it. 'Sarah Isaacs,' and she was an American exchange student at Oxford from NYCU. Only 18 years old when she lost her life. It also showed the coroner's notes and cause of death more graphically, 'postpartum complications after birth.'

She had always dreamed of going to America, but now..., knowing her mother had passed away, and so tragically, it made her hold back a little. She wanted to take time to digest everything, to find more facts and tangible leads. She began with submitting a DNA test and spending a considerable time researching and analysing her newfound genetic connections.

After her years studying at Oxford, and then travelling in gap years on exotic adventures with her friends, Jackie decided it was now or never. Ready to escape the boredom of her dead-end job, she applied to be a summer camp leader for a season at Timberlake West Camp in New York's Catskill Mountains, USA. Now, with a new sense of purpose in her step, she strode off ready to face her demons. She roped in her lovely boyfriend William and together they embarked on the chance of a lifetime for a young couple.

The kids at summer camp were amazing and they loved Jackie and Will. The scenery was magnificent, awe-inspiring. By day they made camp and cooked on campfires, fishing and hunting, abseiling, and canoeing, sailing and boating or wake boarding and wake surfing off the speedboats on the crystal lakes. Everyone making new friends and enjoying group activities, and team challenges, like treasure trails and obstacle courses. They absolutely loved it, and by night they had cookouts and songs and quizzes around the campfire. In no time they were just one big happy family.

They loved the kids and were always there to wipe away the tears from an insecure or homesick child or give them a hug and reassurance. One such little girl was 'Sarah Pinna.' She had just had a good night call with her mom, but her older brother Zach was calling her a baby. "A big cry-baby! Don't be such a big cry-baby!" he yelled at her and made her cry all the more.

Little Sarah reminded Jackie so much of her childhood self. She cradled her, wrapped in her favourite pink unicorn fleecy blanket and made comforting sounds to calm her.

The moment was so poignant for Jackie, a moment her own mother was never to experience, never to be there to comfort her own little child when Jackie could have been her 'little princess.' As tears filled her eyes, little Sarah hugged her "Don't be sad!" Sarah said tapping her hand soothingly.

Jackie had resolved to find out more and she would. She had her DNA results. When summer camp was over she could work in New York City. She had a six-month work visa, she could do it.

As always happens, their brilliant times at summer camp came to an, all too soon, end. As the happy campers said their 'farewells' little Sarah brought Jackie a parting gift. "This is a special notepad and pen, for your 'wishes.' It has our address and phone numbers on the inside cover. You can, No! You must! Call me any time and if you want to come visit you must. We love you!! We miss you already!!!xxxx"

Sarah and Zach Pinna's mother began loading their bags and paraphernalia into the car. "These guys sure do think the world of you!" their Mom said, "Come over and see us when you are in New York, we're in the village!"

"I might just take you up on that. I've applied for a couple of temporary PA and Events Management jobs in NYC. May as well use my degrees." "Great!! Keep in touch. I'll call you too!" she smiled and waved as she drove off, the children waving frantically from the open car windows.

When the Pinna family arrived back in Manhattan their mother was so impressed with all she heard about Jackie, she called her…

"My children are telling me I am in desperate need of a PA and Events Manager, if you would be interested in a coming over for an interview?! I really am rushed off my feet and it would be a godsend to spend more quality time with my husband and the family. Could you help organise our lives and keeping the children in check?" she quizzed, smiling to herself.

The interview went amazingly well. The Pinna's Manhattan penthouse apartment was absolutely fabulous and overlooking Central Park. They had a beach house in the Hamptons, a winter lodge in Aspen, a mega-yacht in the Caribbean and a fabulous beach house in Bel-Air. Plus, three boisterous children, a lot to organise. Fresh coffee arrived.

"More coffee Jackie?... My mother's name was Jacqueline you know. Everyone called her Jackie too!" said Rita passing Jackie a steaming coffee.

"My mother's name was Sarah." said Jackie.

"My older sister's name was Sarah; I named my daughter after her. 'Sarah Isaacs,' we lost her when she was 18 years old. You remind me of her so much, soo mm- much!" Rita Isaacs-Pinna said her voice trailing away to a whisper.

"Ohhh!!" Jackie gasped in sympathy. Not the time for disclosures. A time to find more answers.

Instinct told Jacqueline maybe there was more to this serendipity than meets the eye. She felt so near to her birth mother, to be in her mother's country, in New York, near to where she was born and lived for most of her 18 short years. Not so much a resolution, maybe it was... but maybe it wasn't, not the time to jump to conclusions. But who knows where the search may lead. This was more a time to end those years of not knowing and pretending. The silent acceptance of who she really is, a good person. The time to release those hidden demons and pretence and start believing in herself and something new and very real and wonderful.

Cider

Brent Kelly

A brew of orchard bric-a-brac
that brims with pip and pith and skin.
A frothless broth a jackdaw's chack
it holds the autumn mist within.

A stormy gold September hue
a moony scent of rainfall drops.
Of crabby apples old and new
nostalgia scattered windfall crops.

Now shades of life are autumn glazed
the warming rituals lie ahead.
A heritage of glasses raised
from bowls of amber russet red.

A frumpy scrumpy viscous crunch
A snooty fruity apple punch

Treasure Flowers - *Gazania*
Creana Bosac

Treasure flowers in morning sun
remind of moments yet to come
and times gone by, in jewelled display,
amongst the border's rich array.

Radiant blooms rise joyful, bold,
blaze orange-sapphire, citrine, gold,
lift daisy heads of single hue
or compass-striped, burnished anew.

A favourite, 'New Day,' white and rose,
unfurls from border's night repose.
This trove of broaches, glints at sea,
recalls life's riches, found and free.

Brocken Spectre
Chris Rowe

On my horizon once appeared

a Brocken Spectre, rare and weird.

Projected on the cloud ahead,

the creature waved and bowed its head

And greeted me in mimic dance

with rainbowed aura round its stance.

Appearing on a distant peak,

a Brocken Spectre does not speak.

No marsh-meandering Will o' Wisp,

bog-born, misleading through the mist

to lure a wanderer on false ways,

it manifests in mountain haze;

A most companionable wraith

that with the traveller keeps good faith

and cheers them on a rocky climb;

Auspicious visit in good time,

to unexpectedly appear,

a doppelganger bringing cheer.

Northern aurora up on high,

green neon hanging from the sky,

could not have made me feel more blessed

than when the spectre was my guest.

Solstice
Olivia Robinson

Light:

Streaming through the gap in the curtains, hitting the bedroom wall,

late morning.

It creates sunspots on the kitchen floor for the cats on the

stained hardwood floor.

Lean your head back up

bask in the warmth;

temporary pleasure.

Wrestling with time -

Fixed here, for now.

Fighting with the clouds

creating shadows of the walkers and cars.

Shining through the door at work,

guiding me to my place

for now.

Reflecting off of man-made power,

riveted metal and shackled skeletons

parked at odd angles:

The world in reverse

Home:

Breathe in the dew-soaked earth
that is now only just being warmed.
Pinks and golden hues striking the mirror
on the bathroom tiles
for all of five minutes.

My eyes in the strip of light
turn more green than they ever could be
this is my favourite part

In my room
curtains closed
my pupils becoming larger, blacker
darker.
This is fun.
But they shrink to normal size when I go back
in the light.

Fox in a Box
Rita Wilson

'To catch a fox and put him in a box and never let him go.'

Sally could not stop the words going round in her head. She remembered singing them years ago in the church hall wearing her Brownie uniform. They would skip around in pairs singing 'A hunting we will go, a hunting we will go,' until one of them got caught in a box, that was two pairs of hands joined together, then they were out.

The fox before her was trapped in what looked like a box although no-one had actually been a-hunting, they had been fly-tipping. Sally could not understand why if people were prepared to trudge this far with rubbish they could not make the effort to go to the local council tip. The fox had got stuck under a wooden pallet presumably when it had been investigating the content of several black bin bags presumably hoping to find food. The pallet had pinned the poor creature to the ground. It was a bitterly cold morning. The fox was shivering with cold and fear, its pale yellow eyes transfixed on Sally's two year old Jack Russell terrier, Jason.

"Jason, Jason stop that!" commanded Sally as Jason pawed at the pallet. She grabbed his collar and hastily snapped his lead back on. The dog was reluctant to be dragged away from the sad scene and tried to dig his paws into the soggy terrain.

"Right we're going back to the car," Sally told him, pulling hard on the lead. After a few more whelps in the direction of the fox Jason gave in and walked obediently in front of Sally. They reached the car in ten minutes and as if sensing his walk was over for the day, Jason settled in the blanket spread over the back seat.

Sally thought of her friend Gary complaining only last weekend that a fox had got into the hen coop and slaughtered three chickens. It seems they do not kill for food, they kill in excess.

But no, she could not leave the fox in such a predicament. There had been a flurry of snow earlier that morning. In these temperatures it would surely freeze to death. She retrieved some thick gloves that were always kept in the car boot in case, well this was definitely an 'in case' and followed her footsteps back to the clearing.

Pulling on the thick gloves she uttered a few soothing sounds to the fox as she stooped to lift the pallet as high as she could manage. The fox squeezed through the narrow gap and with a flourish of its bushy tail was off in an instant. There was a faint snapping of twigs as it made its way through the woodland. It stopped briefly to look back, either to say thank-you or check it was not being followed. Sally thought the former.

On the way back to the car Sally thought how cruel was the song 'and never let him go.' They had sung it with such glee as they skipped around the hall. The words 'Ding dong bell, pussy's in the well' went through her mind as well as 'The farmer's wife who cut off their tails with a carving knife.' And they say how killing on a computer can seriously affect children's emotions she laughed to herself.

Jason jumped up with delight at the return of his mistress, a pleading look in his eyes. "No, that's enough excitement for one day," said Sally. "We're going straight home."

As she turned the ignition on, Radio Two automatically came on. Slade's 'Merry Christmas Everyone' was blasting out. It was Christmas Day tomorrow and she sincerely hoped that the work Gary had done on reinforcing the hen house would be sufficient.

Moonwalk
Brent Kelly

The sky grows dark the night is new

a passing moon climbs into view

It sizzles as we rendezvous

I watch it for a tick or two

Then pause awhile to let it rise

and race away across the skies

So fleet of foot so old so wise

its milky light a ghostly guise

It guides us through the woodland ways

to light a path in golden sprays

It coats the oaks in gilded glaze

a filmy mist a honey haze

It wanders higher in the blue

to leave behind a silver hue

That fizzles on the midnight dew

I watch it for a tick or two

Everlasting Rose

Creana Bosac

Their rose is in bloom again
this twentieth year,
a single red head curled tight
where it might
one day fail.
But not this year.

Petals intertwined, the heart
bud will open true
to soft patio rain and
silken sun,
fragrant in
shared evenings.

To be sure of evermore
blooms, the groom of long
ago gifts another rose,
single-stemmed in handsome case,
grown real and sealed, clothed,
in the bright silver
celebration
of precious,
everlasting
platinum.

Scenic Route
Cindie Hall

A horse in the meadow

the owner in tow

They're going for a ride

but where they can't decide.

A beautiful sunny day

so plans can delay

To take the scenic route

all the noise on mute.

The sun streams through the overhanging trees

enjoying the warm summer breeze,

The white peppery clouds do tease

but this heat can't be beat.

A hot summer's day

takes all the stresses away.

My Holiday

Anne Knapp

I love this location
it's where I want to be,
a perfect staycation
close to that blue sea.
I love this sandy beach
its golden yellow sands.
I love the little rock pools
where creatures can be found.
I love the ice cream van
my very favourite treat
a double chocolate cornet
there's nothing it can't beat.
I love the fish and chips
that all pervading smell.
Those chunky bits of fish
in their crispy golden shell.
The sky is clear and blue
with not a cloud in sight
I put up my stripy deckchair
then get a sudden fright.
That big scary seagull
has settled next to me.
I pack up in a hurry
it's time for me to flee.

A Fishy Tale
Norma Bowen

"What was that?" said Puff Daddy to the goldfish swimming around him. "I thought I heard a great splash at the other end of the pond." Darting back and forth and looking alarmed the snappers shouted: "We thought we heard something too but forgot all about it. What was it, has something happened?"

Puff Daddy was the eldest of the pond fish and, puffing up his shimmering chest announced in his wise, old voice that the cause of the big splash should be investigated. He summoned all the goldfish to follow him and swam to the north side of the pond. There was much turbulence, which was hard for the fish to swim against, and some of the tiddlers had to turn back.

The investigators hid behind a rock as they fought frothing waves. Puff Daddy whispered to the worried looking goldfish: "Now you lot wait here, I'm going to get closer to see just what is causing this commotion."

He couldn't believe his puffy eyes when he saw a "thing" with an enormous tail thrashing about. He waited until the "thing" calmed down and was resting against a rock. It was part fish and part human.

Puff Daddy waited for a while then bravely but cautiously swam towards it, making sure he had a quick getaway if needed. He called out to the "thing": "Are you all right?" Startled and looking terrified the "thing," which was too tired to swim away, shrunk back against the pond side. "I say again," yelled Puff Daddy, "Are you all right, Who are you, what are you, and what are you doing in our pond?"

Knowing there was no escape the "thing" nervously explained she was a mermaid and a horrible heron had fished her out of the sea but dropped her when it realised she was more than just a fish. "I've never seen a mermaid before," said Puff Daddy, what do mermaids do then?"

"We live in the sea," she explained. "I play most of the time and got lost and came in too far on the tide, when I was kidnapped by that silly bird that can't tell the difference between a mermaid and a fish. My parents will be frantic with worry, they are always telling me to stay in deep water. I expect I'll never see them again." She began to cry and her huge tears plopped into the pond, causing ripples.

Carefully the rest of the goldfish gathered round Puff Daddy. They held an extraordinary meeting, when it was decided that a way had to be found to get the mermaid back to her parents. It was a hard task as the sea was beyond the bottom of the garden and across a field of cows.

"There is no water between us and the sea and none of us can fly, so what can we do?" Puff Daddy asked the meeting. "We have some angel fish," offered one of the floaters. "Yes but we can't fly, we're just fish like you," retorted the most senior angel fish, before mockingly rolling his round eyes at the members. With that the meeting adjourned as it was near lunch time and the fish realised they had to hide the mermaid from the pond owner, who would soon be coming to feed them. Gently they urged the mermaid to follow them to the lily pads, where she was safely out of sight.

The owner appeared and sprinkled rainbow drops into the water and, as the fish quickly darted to get their share of the food, Puff Daddy noticed a garden ornament standing on the pond side. It was shaped like an angel with tremendous wings. Puff Daddy waited until the owner's shadow disappeared from view before swimming to the surface to get a better look at the ornament.

Noticing two beady eyes looking at her through the water, the angel bent forward and said: "Don't you know it's rude to stare!" Puff Daddy was startled but delighted, he thought if it can speak it may also be able to fly. Without further ado, he explained the mermaid's dilemma and begged the angel for help. "I can do that," said the angel pleasantly. "All she has to do is get out of the pond, climb onto my back and 'Bob's your uncle'."

A farewell party was held before the mermaid thanked the fish for their help and blew them kisses as she made a giant, splashy leap onto the back of the angel, who then flew her out into the deep ocean, where she safely swam back to her parents.

The angel ornament returned to her place at the pond side and watched bemused the goldfish swimming round as if nothing had happened. Indeed, the goldfish, which are renowned for having poor memory, had forgotten all about their adventure.

Death is Surprisingly Pleasant

John Trott

My recruitment occurred after a night on the town. I made my unsteady way home having failed, yet again, to pull. I had accepted my fate and anticipated a night in bed, cold, alone, and frustrated, when I bumped into a dark figure.

"So sorry," I burbled, "I wasn't looking where I was going."
"That's not a problem dahling, and where are you going in such a hurry?"
I realised the dark figure was a young woman, her voice resembled that of the old-time actress Fenella Fielding.

She continued, "Why don't we walk together?" She grasped my arm with both hands, leaned into me and rested her head on my shoulder. I could see she resembled Fenella in more ways than one. Her half-exposed breasts blossomed silkily in the soft moonlight.

"Yes, why not," I gulped.

We walked and talked until she led me to a large Edwardian house with an overgrown garden.

"This is where I sleep," she murmured, and taking my hand led me up the garden path to an ornate door.

I followed more than willingly, and we were soon in a dark, old-fashioned room adorned with heavy curtains and a dust-covered bookcase stacked with old leather-bound tomes.

"I'll get you a drink, please relax and take your shoes and coat off," she chuckled, "after all, we have all night."

I couldn't believe my luck and quickly removed my coat, jacket, and shoes and sat on the large, overstuffed settee.

I heard her footsteps behind me, and she leaned over the back, put her arms around my shoulders, and softly nuzzled my neck. The nuzzle turned into a long, drawn-out sucking kiss which progressed into a bite. She had very sharp teeth. I turned and she broke away, handing me my drink.

I noticed she had only one glass. "Aren't you having one?" I queried. "Oh no dahling, I don't drink alcohol, I don't need to."

The glass contained a thick syrupy mixture that eased its way smoothly down my throat and I felt the warmth flowing through my body. I was overwhelmed by feelings of contentment, of strength, and even stronger, of sexual desire.

We made love all night and as we did, she was constantly kissing and biting my neck. I remember thinking I would have to wear a roll-top jumper for at least a week after this.

Eventually, I fell asleep.
When I woke, she was standing looking down at me with a look on her face that brought to mind a cat that has got the cream.

"You are mine now," she murmured, "I own you. I am a vampire and now we have lain together, and I have consumed your blood, we are one and you also are a vampire".

I laughed. "Don't be daft, vampires don't exist."

"If that's what you believe, walk into the hallway and pull the curtain open."

I slipped on my shoes and clothes whilst doubting her sanity. She looked as if she actually believed it and I was thinking, "I'm getting out of here, you're nuts."

I walked out into the hallway and stumbled. I was feeling a little weak and I put that down to my night of sexual excess.

She called from behind me, "I bet you're feeling weak this morning. It's the loss of blood, you need to rest and recover."

I pulled the curtain open and a beam of sunlight dazzled me. It felt as if Mike Tyson had punched me in the face. I was slammed down onto the floor and lay with the sun shining into my eyes. I was feeling progressively weaker and weaker and thought I would pass out.
The curtains closed, apparently of their own accord. "Don't try to get up until you feel stronger. I did warn you."

I must have slept all day and when I awoke it was dark again. She led me back to the sofa. The languid sexuality had been replaced by cold precision and she proceeded to set out the rules I must live by.

"Exposure to sunlight or garlic is harmful to you. If you try to carry on your life in daylight, there are no ifs or buts, you will die. You do not require food or drink but will waste away if you do not drink blood. Human blood is best, but we keep a supply of rabbits for use in emergencies. I have allocated a casket for your use in the cellar. It is fully equipped with the latest Bluetooth equipment, together with loudspeakers and a small screen. You will appreciate these in May, June, and July, they are dreadfully boring months to be a Vampire. Any questions"?

"Yes, the little TV, can I get Sky Sports on it?"

"Oh dahling you do disappoint me, but the answer is yes, you will have Sky Sports and TNT Sports. Now, anything else?"

"So that's it, I just lay in a casket all day watching daytime TV, listen to music and drink rabbit blood?"

She stared at me through half-closed eyelids. "Oh no, we can go out and hunt for young women for you to charm and convert to our way of life. Plus of course, we have each other. We can repeat the experience of last night whenever we want, we can spend our nights making love while drinking each other's blood."

I thought, "Oh well, it beats working nine to five and having no sex life," and happily surrendered.

A Foreseeable Future
Peter Riley

John had been rummaging in the attic of that old cottage, located in the hilly area to the north of the country, that his ancestors had moved to after the apocalypse, and found in the boarded floor a well disguised, small trapdoor. With some difficulty, he lifted the trapdoor. In the compartment beneath was a parcel, preserved by the dry atmosphere of the roof-space. His first thoughts were to tear open the stout brown paper covering, but he hesitated. It had probably been there since the apocalypse so he would have to be careful, as he could not be sure there would be no intruders. He replaced the parcel, closed the trapdoor, and scuffed dust over the surface to hide its outline.

This needed some thought, so he decided to take a walk before preparing his daily meal and consider what to do. The cottage was in a small collection of houses in what had been a farming community. He decided to walk through the woods. It was heavy going, but rather than take the track that led to the next habitation, he would follow the route of his previous wanderings. He knew it unlikely he would meet anyone as the woods were taboo for the few people about.

He was intrigued by the way the trees had grown in a sort of random pattern, except they seemed to be confined by thick lines of thorn trees that bore a white blossom early in the year before the intense heat and then, when the weather cooled, yielded bunches of red berries.

Occasionally he would encounter piles of rusting machinery and heaps of bricks by the side of wide gaps in the line of thorn trees. He had seen this throughout these woods. Probably, he thought, they are boundaries, but why? Perhaps the parcel would have some information.

John's relations had all died of a virus. He had been taught to read by a traveller, who stayed occasionally in the cottage and seemed to have a mission to tell stories of how things were long ago and wanted to pass on his knowledge. John called him his mentor. There were many books in the cottage that gave some information about life as it used to be. He understood that the community was once part of a densely populated country. The cause of the apocalypse was not clear. The traveller seemed to know but was reluctant to tell. His view had been that if you learned to read, you could discover for yourself. John decided to go back to the cottage and open the parcel.

On the way back to the cottage, he mused about what parents and neighbours talked about, what the traveller referred to and what he had picked up from the books. He understood that there had been a time when the land had been densely populated, that people travelled in powered vehicles and lived together in large groups of buildings called cities.

He understood that a plague had killed most of the people who lived in the cities, and those who worked in groups called factories and offices in large buildings. At the same time, the weather had changed so that the temperature rose, causing the sea levels to increase over a short period time. Slowly the civilisation had disintegrated over the whole of the planet as decision makers were the most vulnerable to the plague and people rebelled against the feeble efforts of those left in charge.

Conflict between nations occurred and cities were destroyed by weapons that had lasting destructive characteristics. He was anxious to get back and open the parcel.

At the edge of the wood, he checked the snares in the rabbit warren and found a struggling animal. He lifted it by its long ears and delivered a killing blow to the back of its neck with his work-hardened right hand. Back at the cottage, he revived the stove with wood from the pile. The rabbit was speedily prepared and into a pot of boiling water to produce a stew with vegetables from the garden.

While the pot was simmering, he recovered the parcel from the hide in the attic and carefully unwrapped the brittle paper covering, to reveal a small safe-box. It was not locked and lifting the lid he saw, packed neatly, a line of booklets, each identified on the spine by a decade from 2020 to 2090.

A note enclosed in a transparent envelope lay on top of the booklets. He carefully opened the envelope, took out the note and, after reading, found that the notebooks were the diaries of a lady who had escaped in the year 2091 from her house in a walled estate near the city. She had travelled on horseback with a manservant she called her scarlet pimpernel, to escape from crowds she described as rebels.

Anxious to start researching the booklets, John had a hurried meal, missing the usual draught of mead, cleared the table and laid out the contents of the box. Attached to the note were a couple of sketches, one of the cottages and out-buildings of animal sheds, wagons, and strange mechanical contraptions, some with large wheels and others with metal rakes and blades. The second sketch showed open ground stretching to distant hills and woods, divided into a patchwork of lands enclosed by low hedges of dense bushes. Some of the enclosures had rows of crops whilst others had animals.

At the entrance of the enclosures, there were small brick-built buildings in some and in others, pieces of machinery. He realised that he was looking at an early state of the wooded area he had recently walked, where the hedges were now high thorn trees, and the woods were self-set in unkept enclosures. The cottage had been the centre of a thriving farm. He set up a plan of detailed study of the diaries, clarifying his understanding using the library of books in shelves around the cottage. After some months of study, he uncovered the cause of the apocalypse.

The 2020s had been the kernel of what had been termed a perfect storm, comprising a plague, climate change and political extremism. The plague was called a pandemic, a worldwide virus that multiplied by infecting humans and managed to modify itself to foil all attempts resist it, causing high death rates through lung and heart disease. Medical services were overwhelmed, and fear of contagion had brought international trade to a virtual halt. Industry and commerce were significantly reduced to a low level of small, private enterprises manned by slave labour. At the time of the final diary, seventy years from its first sign, the virus was still claiming lives. The population of the world had been decimated and the birth-rate significantly reduced.

Synchronously, violent changes were occurring to the climate. Summer after summer temperatures were rising, and glaciers and the ice caps were melting. Sea levels rose, permanently submerging fertile lands and islands. People from the inundated lands were crossing borders, escaping to higher levels. Governments worldwide were strengthening border controls but weakening those over manufacture, procurement, quality assurance and medicine due to the shortage of people with experience and wisdom, particularly in governments.

The so-called nuclear states even before the onset of the pandemic were starting to increase their arsenals of advanced weapons. They were now in a frenzy of reorganisation, due to loss of facilities to rising sea levels, reduced numbers of experienced troops and diminished technical knowledge. Pressures of migrating peoples were causing a so-called cold war, with countries mobilising remote nuclear armed vehicles in the air and on land near borders. Failing electronic and informational systems caused by inferior replacements, blamed on reduced regulation and loss of expertise, led to the accidental release of a nuclear weapon and inevitable retaliation, causing a worldwide firestorm.

Most of the capital cities and governments were destroyed and large areas surrounding them were contaminated with radiation. The later diaries described widespread insurrection with mobs raiding rich enclaves but encouraging settlement in remote rural areas. There were signs of regression of the virus, attributed to the radiation in areas around cities and the isolation of people in remote areas.

John now recognised his situation and decided he should follow in his mentor's footsteps and spread his understanding. His village and the surrounding hamlets needed to take a positive attitude and build for a future. He had a duty to encourage growth and, as a matter of urgency, to help build a community.

The Visitor
Norma Bowen

Brothers Gwyl and Hugh Jones and their best buddy, Calvin Stevens, could not wait to begin the school holidays. With the promise of adventure plans were soon under way for the Armine Road kids.

The three lived next door to each other in Fforestfach, a small town in South Wales. In the alleyway that separated the two houses they plotted their course of action. It would begin with a ritual run down steep, Sketty Hill and, with arms akimbo and their jackets billowing in the wind, they would yell: "Watch out Fforestfach."

The boys had been given a long rope of freedom as long as they obeyed the rules, which included: no climbing on the railway wall; no playing football in the street and no scrumping Mr Thomas' apples.

Both sets of parents were fiercely proud of their Welsh blood. With their tongues in their cheeks, it was this special blood, they warned the boys, that gave parents second sight so they would know if the three got up to no good. Fairly street-wise and a bit canny, the boys feigned amazement.

A favourite playground was nearby Gendros Waterfall. It fell into Morriston River, where the boys leapt onto the smooth, grey, stepping stones, which spanned its nearest part.

It was on a particularly hot day, after the boys had waded in the river to cool down and were relaxing on the riverbank, that Calvin, lying with his hands behind his head in deep and serious thought, suggested they expand their skills and climb to the top of the waterfall, normally a no-go area. It was a dangerous place to play as the water cascaded rapidly onto the rocks far below.

Gwyl and Hugh, though unsure about the move, followed Calvin to the crown of the waterfall but refused his further challenge to jump onto a stone a little way from the bank.

Deaf to his friends' pleas, begging him not to jump, Calvin successfully leapt onto the stone. In a triumphant wave of his arms, however, he slipped and fell into the frothing, white swell of water, which swallowed him.

Hours later he was in hospital wired to a life support machine. His parents were devastated with the news that their son was brain dead and a decision to turn off his life support needed to be considered.

Gwyl and Hugh were in shock, as were their parents, who joined Calvin's, mother and father in prayer at his bedside. They stayed all night.

In the early hours of the following morning a man visited them. He brought calm to the room and said his name was Owen Griffiths, a minister of the parish and that he had come to pray with them.

It was later, when the consultant caring for Calvin came to check on him, that the parents realised the minister had gone, surmising that he must have quietly left the room while they were in silent prayer.

A gasp of astonishment from the consultant drew everyone's attention before he incredulously announced that Calvin was breathing unaided. Unbelievable joy filled the room.

Two more doctors were called to examine Calvin. They confirmed he was holding his own, although they could not explain or understand the extraordinary recovery. The consultant said he would remain at Calvin's bedside and advised the parents' to take a break.

On the way to the cafe to have a drink and a little respite they passed the hospital chapel, at the side of which was a brass plaque stating: In memory of Owen Griffiths, Minister of the Parish, 1880-1915.

As one door closes

elsewhere another opens.

Release your pen. Write.

H.T. 2023

Printed in Great Britain
by Amazon

30564505R00085